BROKEN VOWS

The Maliha Anderson Series
A Prequel

BROKEN VOWS

The Maliha Anderson Series
A Prequel

Steve Turnbull

Broken Vows
By Steve Turnbull
Copyright © 2015 Steve Turnbull. All rights reserved.
Paperback Edition, 2017

ISBN: 978-1-910342-75-6

Published by Tau Press Ltd.

Cover art by Ken Preston - kenprestonpublishing.com

For Susan.

i

The Outskirts of Lucknow, India, July 1st, 1857

"You must hurry, Mother."

The sharp crackle of musket fire echoed among the stone buildings. It did not seem close but how was it possible to tell? The young woman watched the others of their party—women and children—disappearing around a corner with their armed escort from the 32nd Regiment.

"I am quite unable to walk in this heat, Barbara, and you are very wrong to demand it of me."

Every empty window was a dark threat. Any of them could be harbouring one of the devilish rebels.

"I am sorry, Mother. Do take my arm," she said in an attempt to console the woman. "Let us move along and catch up with our friends."

"Friends? I have never met such a flock of waspish harridans in all my life."

But she condescended to take her daughter's arm and walk, oh so slowly, along the street. "And you should take care what you say, I am not feeble of mind. Don't you forget it."

"No, mother," she said. "It is not something I will forget."

"Don't you get miss-ish with me, young lady."

Any further admonishing comment was interrupted by the scream of an artillery shell passing overhead. Part of the wall in the house beside them crashed inward and they were showered with shards of stone. There was no explosion.

"My goodness, what a to-do," muttered her mother. The impact did, however, spur her into action. "Stop dawdling, child, let us be on our way."

The journey through the outskirts of Lucknow had seemed interminable. Barbara had wanted to get to the Residency and the safety of its surrounds days before, when the military wives had been evacuated from the camp.

Her mother had refused. She would not believe there could possibly be any danger. The idea of a rebellion did not seem to be a concept she could grasp.

Even after their staff had deserted them yesterday Barbara's mother kept pulling on the rope to summon the maid. Their *ayah* had taken a moment to apologise to Barbara for leaving her. She had said that none of the staff bore her any ill-will but they feared for their own lives if they stayed. Barbara could not blame her, nor the rest of the servants. Being in the employ of her mother was not pleasant, nor particularly well paid. Her parents were notoriously miserly.

Barbara was aware that many native staff remained with their western masters and mistresses and were devoted to them. Sadly her own mother did not have that effect on the servants. Quite the reverse, it seemed.

The kitchen was almost a foreign land to Barbara and breakfast had been a meagre affair.

The repeated cracks of musket fire brought her from her reverie, and she found they were only a short distance from the turn. She cried out in alarm as a bullet churned up the dust barely a foot from her. She looked back; there were renegade *sepoy* in the street behind them. Only a month ago the native troops would have given her no cause to fear but now you never knew if they were going to revolt or be true.

The tales of the terrible massacres at Cawnpore and the defence of Delhi were horrific. Barbara did not even want to hear them; they were simply too monstrous, while her mother seemed to delight in the most appalling gossip, though never thinking it could happen to her.

There was little question about the loyalty of the *sepoy* behind them. They had betrayed their British commanders, perhaps even killed them, and were now part of the force attacking Lucknow. It was just too difficult.

Barbara grabbed her mother and almost pushed her.

They had reached the corner when another shrieking shell passed overhead and struck the building diagonally opposite. Barbara held her breath but nothing happened. She was moving her mother on when the building erupted. The concussion threw her backwards. Her head struck the ground with force and she stared up at the blue sky, awake but curiously insensible.

It seemed as if she was detached from her physical self. She felt no pain. Heard no sound. Could not receive any aroma, pleasant or otherwise.

A man's face appeared over her, mouthing some words. Why did he not speak aloud? As she watched, almost as if he were moving through treacle, he drew his sword and pointed with it back along the street. His mouth opened wide and distantly she heard the word "Fire!"

Distant sharp cracks of musketry.

He reached down and grasped her about the forearm and with a smooth movement pulled her to her feet. Dizziness overwhelmed her and pain throbbed through her skull. She stumbled, barely able to feel her feet. In a trice he had lifted her and thrown her over his shoulder like a bag of grain.

In her dreamlike state she caught a glimpse of half a dozen men, some taking aim, others reloading. She wondered where her mother was.

She took fright when he turned her to face the street behind. A band of mutineers were walking towards them and there, on the ground, was her mother with her eyes closed. Barbara could not tell whether she still lived. The soldier began to move and her mother was out of reach in a moment.

Lifting her head she saw one native fellow pointing his musket directly at her. She saw the smoke of its firing and imagined the bullet on its flight to meet her.

They turned a corner. She woke from her dream, and the sound of battle grew in her ears. The muskets, the screams, the moans. She desperately wished she could not hear it.

Now that her senses had returned she could feel the awful jolting the man was giving her as he stumbled across the debris lying in the streets—it added to the pain in her head.

"Put me down!" she cried.

He did not heed her demand, indeed did not even respond to it. She struggled but he held her all the more firmly. Finally he passed through a gate and deposited her, none too gently, on a wooden bench set in a square of sorts. They were surrounded by buildings on three sides and a wall on the fourth, the one through which they had entered. Soldiers manned every inch of the perimeter.

Now that she was both upright and sensible she examined the man who had taken such liberties with her person. He was tall and dressed in the khaki uniform that some of the regiments now affected. His hair was much the same colour, whether natural or due to bleaching from the strong Indian sun, and in need of grooming.

However there was no time to dilly-dally; her mother must be recovered. Barbara climbed to her feet, pushed past him and made to return through the gate. He reached out and grabbed her arm once more, bringing her to an abrupt halt.

"And where d'you think you're off too, miss?"

That explained it. He was an ill-mannered and low-born Scot. Thankfully he was clean-shaven. Nothing worse than untidy facial hair. His blue eyes were quite appealing but he had a scar across his left temple that was most distracting.

"I am going to fetch my mother. I request you unhand me this instant, my good fellow."

"That'll be Lieutenant to you. Lieutenant Ferguson if you've a mind."

"Well, I haven't and I must fetch my mother. She is an old woman and quite infirm."

"Indeed, Miss…?"

"Though it's little enough of your business, you may refer to me as Miss Flynn."

"Well," he drawled. "Miss Flynn, if you think I'm going to let you walk out of here into a musket battle with artillery flying, then clearly you do not, as you suggested yourself, have a mind."

He pushed her back down on to the bench with so little apparent effort she almost burst into tears. "But I must find my mother."

"Aye, one of the chaps will be along with her very soon."

"But she may be hurt."

At that moment a shell whistled overhead and crashed into one of the buildings behind them. There was a terrible scream from inside. Barbara shivered.

"Would it make you feel better if I went myself and fetched her for you?"

She nodded.

"You promise you'll not follow?"

The scream from the building behind had descended into sobbing. Barbara shivered and nodded again.

"Then I'll be back directly, Miss Flynn."

She remained sitting as he headed through the gate and out into the battle. It was not cold, indeed the weather was exceeding hot, but she held her arms around herself for comfort.

ii

Muchee Bhawan, Lucknow, India, 1st July 1857

The lieutenant was as good as his word and it was only a few short minutes before he returned bearing her mother, cradled in his strong arms.

Barbara stood up and indicated for him to lay the old lady down on the bench. He did so with kind attention and ensured her head did not strike the wood. Then he saluted and headed out once more. Leaving Barbara alone.

She looked around hoping she might see someone who could help her but they were the only civilians in the vicinity. The rattle from the soldiers' muskets was unceasing. She jumped as a huge artillery piece fired its shell on the enemy. The massive gun was mounted on a rampart only fifty yards from where she and her mother rested under a tree. Moments later a second gun, beside the first, roared its defiance. The artillerymen attending the weapons rushed about preparing them for their next shots.

An incoming ball screamed overhead and smashed into the tower. There were many cries and she could hear soldiers shouting vulgarities—and also obscenities—at their unseen foes.

All about her was mayhem.

"Barbara?" her mother's tremulous voice penetrated the constant barrage of chaotic sound.

"I am here, Mother." With a task to focus on Barbara felt the chaos at least pushed to one side. She knelt beside her mother and took her hand.

"Am I dying, child?"

"No, Mother," she said. "I believe you are quite well if a little fatigued."

Another shell shrieked above them but did not strike anything within the small space.

"We have died and gone to Hell."

That was not an unreasonable suggestion, Barbara thought. "No, mother, we are quite alive. But this is most certainly a Hell on Earth."

She had thought the Residency to be much bigger. There were, after all, said to be four hundred civilians and perhaps five or six hundred soldiers and officers. There was certainly not that number here. Nor would they fit.

The soldiers on the wall near the gate set up an intense barrage. The speed with which the muskets were reloaded was quite remarkable; the noise was intense. They appeared to be concentrating their fire into the buildings nearby. There was a disturbance at the gate as both native and European troops tumbled through.

The able-bodied supported those who were injured and many were covered with blood. She stared in horror as she realised the leg of one soldier was completely missing below the knee. His trouser leg was in tatters and blood-soaked. Her stomach turned over and she averted her eyes.

"Close the gate!"

The commanding voice with a Scottish lilt made her look up again. Lieutenant Ferguson made a striking figure framed by the gate arch. He raised his pistol and fired at an invisible enemy. Holstering his weapon, he assisted the men pushing the gates closed.

Once satisfied with the defence he vaulted the debris and went from one injured man to the next. He spoke to each briefly, sometimes with a concerned look on his face and occasionally with a jest.

Shards of stone rained down as a shell struck the tower. The noise was tremendous though the soldiers did not react. Barbara could see countless scars where the walls of the tower had been gouged by the enemy's artillery.

Her mother pressed down on Barbara's shoulder and pushed herself into a sitting position. Barbara was glad to see it; if she could sit up then she could walk.

"Who in the name of damnation are you two?"

The gruff voice belonged to a high-ranking officer dressed in the customary red and white. He sported an impressive and well-maintained moustache, with eyebrows to match. While he was clearly not pleased to see her, she was grateful to be able to speak to someone with authority, even if he was prone to inappropriate language.

She got to her feet. "I am Barbara Flynn; this is my mother. I'm afraid we are stranded here."

He appraised them both for a long moment.

"Major Francis at your service, I'm sure." He gave a slight bow. "I am afraid we cannot offer you any comforts or hospitality. This is a most inopportune time. We will be retreating to the Residency presently, Miss Flynn, and will have no time for dawdlers."

"My mother is somewhat infirm. She cannot walk far or with any speed."

"I can keep up with you, girl."

"Yes, mother."

Her mother coughed with the heat and dust in the air.

"You can ride on the supply truck," said the major.

"Thank you."

Barbara had got the impression from his words that departure would be soon but that turned out not to be the case at all. The afternoon wore on. The sun's heat blasted down and the twisted tree they sheltered beneath provided little shade.

And her mother complained almost without let-up. The only time she was not expressing her dislike of the heat, the noise, the smells, the shouts and the screams was when she was coughing. And then, when she regained her breath, she complained about that.

Barbara was used to it but there was a considerable difference between listening with half an ear to her mother's complaints while engaged in some detailed embroidery, and enduring it in the heat of the day and the midst of a battle.

About three o'clock the lack of food and water became too much.

There were numerous natives about the place but events had made her nervous about speaking to them. And the only European to whom she had been introduced was Lieutenant Ferguson. He would have to do.

"Be still, Mother," she said. "I will see if I can find us some water at least."

She stood and brushed down her skirts. They were covered in masonry dust and, no doubt, smelt of gunpowder. Looking around she had little difficulty in spotting the dominant figure of Lieutenant Ferguson engaged in firing his musket from the top of the wall. He had a native beside him who was assisting in reloading.

Studying the route to him she saw it would entail some clambering as there was no direct path. So be it. She lifted the hem of her dress and made her way across the open area. She barely jumped when a projectile slammed into the ground twenty yards from her. The attack had been constant for hours and she had felt herself becoming inured to the constant barrage.

Fallen masonry had been arranged into a semblance of steps up the banks to the wall. She found, as she gained height towards the top of the wall, the volume of the musket fire increased. The soldiers stood behind the ramparts and fired into the city. She was curious to see beyond the parapet but when one of the men further along jerked and collapsed into the dirt with a red trail tracking down his face, eyes staring, she kept her head down. She was sure she would have been sick if she had recently eaten.

She finally reached Lieutenant Ferguson's position. The native was wide-eyed at the sight of her.

"Gun!" shouted the lieutenant. He held the spent musket out but did not cease in scanning the scene outside the walls. His man did nothing but stare at Barbara. "Gun!"

Barbara moved up and took the musket from the lieutenant's hand. It was considerably heavier than she expected. She then relieved his man of the loaded weapon and placed it against his open palm. He groped slightly and his hand brushed against hers.

He gripped hard, crushing her fingers and making it impossible for her to release the weapon. His head jerked around.

"Miss Flynn, what the deuce do you think you're playing at?"

iii

He did not release her fingers. A musket ball struck the stonework beside his head showering them both in dust.

"Please, Lieutenant, do keep your head down."

He stepped down but still did not let go of her hand.

"You are telling me to keep my head down, Miss Flynn?" he said. "Perhaps you would like to take my place? I'm sure you could rout the enemy with a single shot."

"There really is no cause to take that tone, Lieutenant. I was merely concerned for your safety."

"This is a war, Miss Flynn, and taking part entails certain risks."

It was at this moment he seemed to notice he had her hand enfolded in his own. He slipped his fingers up the barrel a few inches and relieved her of it. She rubbed her fingers. He looked at her as if expecting her to speak but she felt awkward. In the face of the events taking place here on the wall, her need for food and water had become quite insignificant.

"I take it you came here for a reason other than wanting a better vantage point."

"Yes, of course."

"And that is?"

Barbara cleared her throat. "We have no water or food."

If he had been angry or exasperated she would have had something to push against. As it was he simply stared at her, almost as if she had not spoken at all.

She felt as if she needed to explain. "It is exceeding hot. My mother and I have been travelling since this morning."

"And you expect me to get it for you?"

"No, of course not, but you are the only person other than Major Francis that I know."

There was a momentary lull in the attack. The constant crack of musketry reduced to the occasional shot—less than one every few seconds.

He blew out a long breath he had apparently been holding and nodded. He turned to the Indian. "Ram, take Miss Flynn here and introduce her to the Quartermaster."

"Yes, sir." The man set off back the way Barbara had come and without thinking she turned to follow.

"Miss Flynn?"

She turned back. "My apologies for disturbing you." She hesitated as she looked into his eyes. "Thank you."

"I was just going to say that, in future, I do not recommend approaching a battleground. I have warned you twice now, perhaps you would consider taking my advice?"

She nodded and took off after Ram.

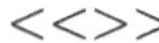

"This is really most unpleasant," said her mother as she swallowed the last of the rice with a small quantity of white meat—Barbara thought it might have been chicken—along with some unidentifiable green vegetables mixed in. They had been forced to use their fingers the way the natives did.

The water was warm but she was grateful for it. Her mother had drunk rather a lot of it but Barbara did not begrudge her. She needed all her strength for the rest of the journey. The QM, Major Winthrop, had stated it was not far to the Residency but it was a journey through the city streets and the mutineers could be hiding anywhere.

The sun was descending towards the horizon. The fighting dropped off a little in the early evening and as the darkness drew in it became impossible to see the enemy. The British stopped firing and most of the men—those that still lived—came down from the walls.

The enemy, however, knew exactly where this small garrison stood so their artillery continued to fling shells while their soldiers still fired their muskets. There was no let-up in the attack, only a slight reduction in its intensity.

The men gathered in groups around small fires. The evening was as hot and close as the day, but there was something comforting about a fire. Barbara looked longingly at the soldiers as they ate, drank, talked and laughed around their homely camp-fires.

"Would you and your mother care to join my men, Miss Flynn?"

Ferguson's voice at her shoulder made her jump. She had not even known he was there in the dark, watching her.

"I'm sure your offer is well meant, Lieutenant," she said. "But I doubt your men would appreciate two women at their fire."

"That is considerate, Miss Flynn," —she could tell from his tone he was laughing at her— "but it would be far worse to allow you to suffer here alone. They can tolerate a few hours of minding their language."

Barbara had opened her mouth to protest once more but her mother interrupted.

"Stop your silly whining, Barbara. I wish to sit by the fire."

Which settled the matter and a place was made for the two of them round a fire with a dozen common soldiers, and a lieutenant.

While the conversation did not flow, neither did the men stint on drinking their bottled beer. They offered one to Barbara from a misplaced sense of honour which she declined politely. And she was horrified when her mother accepted. They even passed her a tin mug so that she did not need to drink it from the bottle.

"Mother, what are you doing?" she hissed.

"Oh hush, Barbara."

Barbara did as her mother told her, but fumed quietly at such common behaviour.

"So, Lieutenant Ferguson," she said. "I understand the Fergusons are an important Scottish family. How is it you are not with a Scottish regiment?"

"That would be a clan rather than a family, Miss Flynn. But no, I am not of the clan chief's family."

"Oh," she said ineffectively. Her next question was not one that could be asked. If he was just a commoner himself, how could he have possibly bought his commission?

"Have some of the beer, Barbara," said her mother.

"No, thank you, Mother."

She managed to avoid any further improper suggestions from her mother as a runner came around and spoke briefly in Lieutenant Ferguson's ear. She noted with some satisfaction that the lieutenant was not drinking.

"Prepare for the retreat, gentlemen," he said in a low voice. They all stood, except Barbara and her mother. "Leave the fire alight. We don't want to give the idea something is happening."

The soldiers disappeared into the dark.

"Mrs Flynn, do you and your daughter have your orders in regard to the retreat?"

Barbara knew her mother had no answer. "Major Francis said we should go on the supply vehicle?"

"That makes sense. Good."

"But I have not seen any beasts for pulling such a thing, where would we find it?"

In the flickering light of the fire she saw him smile. "Look out for a puffing billy."

"A steam vehicle?"

"We are quite modern."

iv

Lieutenant Ferguson still felt himself to be in a state of shock at the idiocy of the Flynn girl. To come up on to the parapet like that was the height of stupidity, though he had to smile. Yes, it was stupid in one respect but such single-mindedness did deserve some credit—even if it was likely to get her killed in short order.

But she had listened to him. And, of course, she had succeeded in her intention—she had got some food for herself and her mother. What a creature the mother was. He would not tell the daughter but the mother had put up far more of a fight when he first hoisted her up. He did not envy the girl such a mother, or any future husband such a mother-in-law.

Now why had he thought that?

A head popped up in the building across the way and he fired. The head disappeared, but he was unsure whether he had hit his target. Fighting in a city like this was unlike anything he had experienced. The enemy could be close enough to speak with as they fired at one another across a street.

A runner came up and told him that Major Francis required his presence.

Lieutenant Ferguson backed down from the wall and made his way to where the major stood with his aide. The lieutenant came to attention and saluted, the major's salute was casual.

"We need to prepare to blow the place to pieces, Lieutenant," he said. "Look after that will you?"

"After all the work we've put in to fortifying it, sir?"

"Sir Lawrence's orders, and we can't leave the place in the hands of the rebels."

"Very good, sir."

He was right of course. The *Muchee Bhawan* overlooked the Residency ground far too well. With the enemy occupying the tower, especially after their improvements, they would command complete control of the Residency.

"Have a word with the engineers and decide how much powder we should leave behind. Anything we can't take with us—and that includes the eighteen pounders—must be completely destroyed."

So they didn't fall into enemy hands either, but it seemed such a shame to destroy a pair of such beautiful artillery weapons.

"Yes, sir. Anything else?"

"And we've got a couple of civilians—women. Make sure they don't get left behind, will you?"

"Miss Flynn and her mother?"

"You've met them? Good," he said. "Well, that's about it. The retreat will be at midnight."

Lieutenant Ferguson saluted again and headed towards the tower. He commandeered a couple of the *sepoy* then gathered the engineers, sappers and artillerymen that could be spared.

The guess was that they would need to ignite the majority of their powder reserves, over two hundred barrels. The only bulk transport they had was the billy with its Faraday trailer and there was a limit to what it could carry.

They set to work moving the barrels into the cellar below the main tower. They had no way of signalling back to the Residency as their telegraph device had been shot to pieces within minutes of mounting it. It had been almost as bad for the Residency equipment: they had just enough time to get the message through before a storm of musketry ripped the wooden arms and pulleys to pieces.

The *Muchee Bhawan* garrison had to hope the Residency staff would assume they had received the message and set up a diversion. It was less than five hundred yards to the gate of the Residency but that was through city streets that would become a shooting gallery if the enemy knew what they were about.

They stacked all the powder they could into the lower cellar and then added more in the upper levels—they would be less effective there but there was simply no room below. One of the sappers suggested packing the gaps between the gunpowder casks with musket shot, of which they also had considerably more than they could take.

Unfortunately they had spent the last three weeks building up both the quality of the defences and the munitions available. That Sir Lawrence should have them withdraw at the last moment was not entirely understandable, but he was the commanding officer.

The musket ball plan was not practical in the end so instead they put a wall of musket ball barrels around the gunpowder. The intention was that the explosion would drive the balls outward and add to the destructive power. At the very least they must bring down the tower.

Ferguson found himself in an argument with the artillerymen who were very reluctant to leave their guns. He would have suggested they try pulling it themselves—since they had evacuated all the livestock and artillery horses—unfortunately he suspected they might have considered that a serious option. In the end he simply had to override them.

On the other hand he gave them *carte blanche* to use as many shells as they wished against the enemy for the afternoon and evening. This seemed to please them since their beloved guns would wreak considerable havoc before being destroyed.

As evening drew in he discussed the triggering mechanism with the sappers and engineers. The only practical solution was a long fuse which meant someone would have to light it. They had enough for a five-minute fuse if it was laid carefully. He had them lay three fuses of equal length instead, giving slightly over a minute.

He reported to the major and volunteered to ensure the tower was destroyed.

The major gave him a serious look. "The tower must come down, Lieutenant, and the guns thoroughly disabled."

"I understand, sir."

The major looked at him. "Yours was a field promotion, was it not?"

"Yes, sir."

"Any particular reason you're not in a Highland regiment?"

"I am one of three that escaped with our lives, sir."

The major nodded. "I've heard the story. You're a good man, Ferguson. You don't have to give your life. We would have no shortage of volunteers."

"I'm not planning on dying yet, sir."

The major shook his hand.

v

Barbara marvelled at how smoothly the retreat was carried out.

The main guns continued to launch their barrage regularly through the evening while the majority of the men gathered in the central space. They lined up in neat rows and Barbara was surprised at the total number—and there were still those manning the walls.

The smaller guns were broken down by the artillerymen and their wheels wrapped with cloth so they made no sound on the stones. They were assigned a dozen natives each to pull them. No animal could possibly have tolerated the tremendous noise and explosions.

The puffing billy emerged under its own steam from the bottom of the tower. Not only were its metal wheels similarly muffled but there were wrappings around its pistons. There was considerable activity while it was attached to a trailer stacked high with barrels of munitions, sacks of rice and other foods. It looked like an outrageous pile, and it was quite obvious the billy was not large enough to pull it. Barbara wondered whether they had rather over-estimated its capabilities.

Meanwhile, a group of soldiers had been deployed to clear the piled up defences from the around the gate, otherwise they would not have been able to get any of the wheeled vehicles out.

Barbara guided her mother to the trailer and, with some considerable effort and false starts, managed to get them both into a comfortable position sitting on it. Her mother had clearly imbibed too much beer and immediately slept.

With the trailer carrying so much powder, Barbara tried not to think what might happen if one of the enemy's exploding shells happened to land on it. Most likely she would know nothing about it until she found herself in His presence.

At some signal, of which she was not aware, the gates opened and the men began to file out. They did not march but walked with as little noise as possible. Within the confines of the walls it seemed they made a great deal of noise, but here their footfalls echoed and re-echoed.

Lieutenant Ferguson went past towards the tower rather than the gate. "Lieutenant?"

He paused and looked up to where she sat on a barrel of powder.

"Taking the risks in your stride, Miss Flynn?"

"Are you not coming with us?" Her words came out a little more plaintive than she had intended.

"I will be following on a little later."

Her heart leapt at the only conclusion she could think of. He, and a few volunteers no doubt, would remain in the garrison to give the impression it was still manned. Such a brave sacrifice. "May I say it has been a pleasure knowing you."

"Thank you, Miss Flynn. Am I to consider myself forgiven then?"

"Of course, you were only doing your duty."

"You are too kind, lass." He saluted.

She bit her tongue; she would not remonstrate with him for such a familiarity if he was giving his life for others so nobly.

"Now if you'll excuse me, I have some duties to attend to."

"Most certainly. Don't let me keep you."

He strode away. The billy puffed more strongly and without any warning she felt as if she were falling. She threw her arms out to catch herself but found she was still seated on the barrel.

She had never experienced a Faraday but this must be one. It explained why they had overloaded the trailer with so much, and how the small vehicle would be able to pull it. Sir Michael Faraday's invention was used extensively by trade people wishing to transport large quantities of material as easily as half the amount. The device made things light.

Her mother snored, though not in as laboured a manner as usual, from where she lay propped up against a barrel of salt beef. She had missed the whole experience which was, perhaps, just as well as she might well have made a loud fuss that the enemy would have heard.

The billy's muffled panting increased in frequency and there was a gentle jerk as it pulled the trailer into motion. It was only a few seconds later the billy went under the gate arch followed by the trailer. The light from the various fires had provided some illumination within the fort but out on the street there was almost no light. For which, Barbara realised, they should be grateful. Even the moon had yet to rise.

The only sound she could hear was the panting of the billy. And that sounded loud indeed. The billy had been the last to leave the fort, and she knew why. It was the one thing in their column likely to attract attention so, to give the soldiers the best chance of getting to the Residency, it was left to last.

And they were on it.

Once more it was the best option. It was a humbling experience to realise that she and her mother were of no value to the major. In truth they were a liability.

The billy continued to trundle through the streets. They seemed to reach a high point on one of the roads, and looking out behind she could see flashes of artillery fire that created silhouettes of the buildings for a moment. She had no way of knowing whether it was the enemy's artillery or their own.

Then the world went white. At first she thought it to be the flash of nearby artillery, but the light did not stop. She craned her neck and in the middle distance she saw the tower of the fort lit up brilliantly. Great flames erupted from the fort and the tower trembled.

A billowing cloud of smoke rose into the air, its underside glowing from the light of the explosion. And as the light died the thunderous roar rolled over them. The tower wavered then crumbled as if its base had been removed. It descended vertically and another cloud went up.

The fall of the tower obliterated the remains of the explosion and all the light went out. But, moments later, the death rattle of the tower thundered across them.

Her mother snored.

Barbara stood with her hand at her throat. Lieutenant Ferguson had succeeded in destroying the fort. What a brave man. He would be remembered.

She sat down again, her heart torn asunder, and she did not know why.

Lieutenant Ferguson watched the billy and its trailer bump across the debris-covered ground and out through the gate, leaving him alone. Within the walls the billy's puffing had echoed back and forth but once it was outside the sound of it faded into the thumping of the artillery from the Residency. They had started their diversion.

He checked his pocket watch. It was five past midnight. He should give the troops a few minutes to get clear. The *Muchee Bhawan* was strangely quiet. He sat on the very bench that she had been sitting on all afternoon. He remembered how she had felt when he picked her up. For a moment he had thought she was dead but then she moved. Her eyes were unfocused but beautiful. Deepest brown, and her hair the colour of chestnuts in autumn.

Not that they had autumn here, at least not the autumn he was used to.

He cursed himself; he was getting maudlin. And in ten minutes he could be dead: either shot by the enemy or blown to pieces because he had to get close enough to ensure the gunpowder went off. Well, if that happened he would join his compatriots.

He looked at his watch again. Only a minute had passed.

He stood and listened. He could no longer hear the billy. Just the distant crackle of muskets and the thump of the artillery. Musket fire could not be distinguished but the artillery was theirs by the sound of it.

The East India Company regiments controlled India, or they thought they did. Coming from Scotland, Ferguson understood what it was like to have an invading force take over your country and try to wipe your history clean. It was what the English had tried to do to his homeland, and what the Company wanted to do to India.

And the Indians objected just as the Scots had. It was before his time, of course, but the memories were still fresh in the old men, and they hated the English.

Yet here he was on the side of the invaders. He smiled ruefully at no one and wondered what the old men would think of him now. The whys and wherefores were in the past. When he had joined up it was for adventure and because he was the third son of a farmer with no prospects.

Given what he knew now perhaps he would have chosen some different course: the Americas or perhaps Australia. But if wishes were horses the beggar would ride. He was here and there were people that needed protecting.

Two more minutes had passed. Two minutes for the fuses to burn and they should be far enough away. Then he heard voices. The language was not English. They were still outside the wall but if no one fired at them they would soon get bold enough to enter.

He had better light the fuse now.

He made his way to the tower as silently as he could manage. He felt in his pocket for the box of matches he had been given by one of the sappers. "I'll be looking to get them back." He had said.

Someone shouted.

Lieutenant Ferguson located the end of the three fuses. He took out his revolver and laid it on the ground next to him. He might have to defend the position. He opened the tin of matches and extracted one. If the enemy were in the compound they would see him when he lit up, because the magnesium in the tip burned very brightly.

He couldn't light the fuse without it. So he struck it.

The flare dazzled him for a moment. He should have shut his eyes. There was an increase in the shouting and the crack of a musket. The ball pinged off a stone near him. He focused on the task in hand and touched the match to the fuses. They burst into flame in a cloud of smoke and sparks. He dropped the still-burning match and grabbed up his revolver.

Another half-dozen musket shots went off. He expected to be hit but there was only a tug across his shoulder as a ball went through his jacket. He rolled to the side so he was no longer silhouetted by the flames. He glanced back and saw with satisfaction that all three fuses were burning steadily.

Once more dazzled, he could not see any of his assailants. He got into a crouch and headed in low, long strides towards the gate. Something moved ahead of him and he fired without really seeing it.

He heard the bullet ricochet off the stone but there was no cry of pain.

If they knew what was good for them they would be running like the blazes themselves. No one shot at him as he ran through the gate. With gun in his hand and oblivious to anything else, he ran as if all the demons of Hell were biting at his heels. He stumbled but managed to keep himself upright.

The world behind him erupted. The sound washed across him and the force of the blast knocked him to the ground. He struck the stones heavily. He rolled over on to his back and watched a ball of smoke and flame billow upwards into the sky.

The whole area was lit up bright as day for long seconds. The expanding fireball took in the buildings in the immediate vicinity of the *Muchee Bhawan.* The walls around it crumbled pierced by a million explosion-driven musket balls. The surrounding buildings crumbled too. The tower above him wavered. If it fell the wrong way he would be a dead man.

But it did not fall in any direction. It simply crumpled and collapsed like a house made of cards. A hundred tons of stone roared as it crashed down and extinguished the fire. Everything went black.

The air filled with dust and smoke. Lieutenant Ferguson coughed. He pulled out a kerchief and tied it around his face, climbed to his feet and stumbled towards the Residency.

vii

The Residency, Lucknow, India, July 2nd, 1857

It was a curious thing but she had somehow expected cheers when their column arrived at the Residency. She had hoped for some sort of friendly greeting at least. Perhaps just someone who could tell them what they should do, where they could find rooms, and all the little things that must be done now they had reached the safe haven.

The first thing that struck her about the Residency, since there was not a great deal to see in the dark, was the smell. No, the word "smell" did not do justice to the appalling stench of rotting flesh that struck her as she entered the gate. It made her feel sick and she imagined it was the thing that awoke her mother at that particular time.

It was still the middle of the night, not even half past midnight. There were no cheers and no welcoming committee. The soldiers had already been dispatched to their billets; she could make out some of them disappearing into the nearby buildings. She stayed aboard the trailer as the billy dragged it through the tangle of debris.

"Where are we?"

"We have reached the Residency, Mother."

"I feel strange."

"We are on a Faraday device."

"Devil's work," her mother muttered then fell silent again.

Barbara wondered if her words had confused her mother, but then the woman snored. Barbara took out the bottle of water and brought it to her lips. There was a long pause, the weight of it said it was not empty and yet nothing came out. She had just pulled it away from her lips when *something* came from the neck of the bottle. It glistened like water but moved like, she was not sure, thick custard?

A large globule formed and fell slowly. She tried to jerk away but it struck her dress. It did not splash but seeped into the material. She touched it and it made her fingers wet like water. She tried to smell it but nothing could penetrate the miasma of the Residency.

Finally she touched it to her mouth and tasted nothing. It was water. Then she remembered the stories people told of how the Faraday made things fall slowly and liquids behave so strangely. She tipped up the bottle again and sucked the strange water into her mouth and swallowed it.

The driver of the billy seemed to know where he was heading. She could see him and the stoker silhouetted by the light of the furnace. The billy proceeded along a road and took a left turn at a post office. Soldiers stood at its door watching them pass.

They continued deeper into the Residency. Although there was a single Residency building, the term also encompassed the whole residential and administrative area, surrounded by a wall and individual buildings including two hospitals—one for the natives—the church and the homes of richer families.

The billy came out between a house and some sort of municipal structure. There was a lawn stretching out, she could not make out what the lumps on it were, and beyond it the Residency itself. The billy drove round the lawn and eventually came to a halt near a building where the smell of rotting flesh gave way to that of live animals. Her weight suddenly returned and she almost overbalanced before she had a chance to adapt.

After the destruction of the tower there had been quiet, but now the enemy guns spoke again, both artillery and muskets. She heard crashes as the round shot impacted the buildings and thuds as they struck the ground and bounced. Every now and then there would be an explosion.

The constant barrage was unnerving. It was as if there was no safety and at any moment she could be struck. The contemplation of her mortality reminded her of the heroic bravery of poor Lieutenant Ferguson. It saddened her to think he had given up his life simply to ensure that the enemy did not gain control of the fort or the weapons within it.

There was a child crying.

She looked around. They must find a room where they could rest but perhaps tonight they might just remain here. The air was warm, and her mother was resting contentedly. Barbara wondered whether there was a supply of beer she could acquire in order to keep her mother satisfied. Clearly being married to her father had not completely expunged her mother's origins. Barbara admonished herself for having such unkind thoughts.

The trailer creaked as it settled beneath the full weight of its load. The stoker closed up the door of the furnace, and Barbara wondered what he had been doing—perhaps furnace fires needed to be banked just as those in houses before they could be left safely. He jumped down and headed into one of the buildings.

They were alone.

A shell went over and crashed to the ground nearby. She could not see it but the noise must have woken more children as there was a sudden increase in infant weeping sounds.

Barbara was not sure how she could sleep in this but, as her eyes adjusted to the deep darkness, she moved along the trailer near her mother and settled down with her head resting on a bag that smelled of gunpowder.

Having regained his feet after the destruction of the tower, Lieutenant Ferguson made his way into the Residency and reported to Major Francis.

"Any difficulty, Lieutenant?"

"None, sir."

"Job well done, I will mention your name when I report to Sir Lawrence."

"Thank you, sir."

"Your men have been stationed at the Judicial Garrison, do you know where that is?"

"I know the Judiciary building, sir."

"All right then, carry on."

He saluted then headed past the barracks and to the east.

viii

The battered Judiciary, now fortified, overlooked a swathe of the city which had previously been home to the natives. Unlike some parts of the Residency the buildings opposite did not come right up to the walls; there was some open ground between them. It made it less attractive as an attack point and so his troop would be able to hold it with relative ease.

The top of the building was blasted and tattered by artillery fire but they still mounted a watch up top. His second lieutenant, Brassie, had made sure he had his own place to sleep in the heart of the building, under the main stairs.

"Welcome back, sir."

"Thanks, Brassie."

"Certainly made some fireworks."

"Aye, it was quite a sight."

"Did you manage to kill any of the bastards?"

"Not sure, some might have got caught."

"Let's hope you did," said Brassie, then he grinned. "That was a pretty bit of skirt that come in."

"Miss Flynn, you mean?"

"Bet she'd keep a bloke warm on a cold night, don't ya think, sir?"

"I think that's an entirely inappropriate way to discuss the lady."

Brassie said nothing further. So he climbed into his small space and fell asleep.

It seemed like he'd only just shut his eyes when Brassie was shaking him awake.

"Five o'clock, sir."

"All right, get to your bed."

Brassie disappeared. Four hours' sleep should be plenty for anyone, Ferguson thought while he eyed his blanket. The air was still stifling hot; this time of year in India it barely cooled down at night. At least the flies weren't so active in the dark.

He took the stairs up three flights to the top of the building and checked the guards. Then went through each floor making sure he understood the layout and the location of the men.

Finally he checked the cellars. He pressed his ear against the stone wall closest to the perimeter. There was nothing. It was early days but there was no doubt the enemy would start to drive mines through from the buildings opposite. As long as they checked regularly they should hear the digging.

That duty completed, he headed out while the sun was not yet up.

He was not fully familiar with the layout of the Residency nor the distribution of the regiments through the various buildings that marked the edge.

He went north, past the post office, to the artillery battery beside the hospital and then along the wall around the back of the Residency. He was grateful it was not his men that were assigned this position. Not only was it exposed to the weather with very little cover, it was one of the most accessible points for the enemy to fire into the compound.

The church stood to the north-west in a very exposed position. He checked inside and found it had been converted to a grain store. He headed south towards the next group of buildings and found the billy—its furnace now cold—still loaded with Miss and Mrs Flynn asleep among the barrels of food and munitions.

"We'll make a soldier o' you yet, Miss Flynn."

She blinked open her eyes. The hazel eyes and red-blond hair were pitched at an angle and grinning at her.

"Lieutenant Ferguson?" She sat up abruptly and her head swam. "I thought you were dead."

"Is that so? And why, pray, might I be visiting with the angels?"

"The explosion."

"Aye, it was quite exciting, wasn't it? Two hundred barrels of powder will make a pretty bang." He laughed. "You thought I'd given my life for the garrison?" He looked a little more thoughtful. "If it were required, then I would. But we do have such a thing as a slow fuse. I'm not one for wasting my life, I quite enjoy living it."

Barbara looked around, her mother was still asleep. The sun was up but not yet high enough to cast its light into the streets. There was the crackle of musketry in the distance.

She wondered how she would get down with any dignity. The trailer bed was a good four feet above the ground and there were men—Europeans and native—unloading the goods that had been transferred during the night.

Lieutenant Ferguson spotted her plight and raised his arms, offering to carry her down. There was no choice in the matter. It was most embarrassing. She sat on the edge, he placed his hands on her waist and she pushed herself off. She landed so lightly it was as if he had his very own Faraday device.

She adjusted her dress, belatedly realising she must be in a terrible state. She had been wearing the same things for a whole day. Even slept in them.

"Am I to suppose you wept over my doom, Miss Flynn?"

"Only as much as I would consider it a sad, if honourable, fate for anyone."

He bowed and turned to leave.

"Lieutenant Ferguson?"

He turned back. "Miss Flynn?"

"I want to thank you for your consideration and assistance over the last day."

"You're welcome, of course." He turned away again.

"If I may trouble you a little more?"

"Of course, Miss Flynn." He stood quite stiffly as if he really did not wish to be there.

"I do beg your pardon, and I am sure you have much more important matters to which you must attend, however my mother and I know nobody here. As you know we have nothing and we do not know who we can speak to about lodgings and perhaps clothes and other necessaries."

His stance softened somewhat.

"All the best accommodations have been taken," he said. "As has almost every other inch of space. We have hundreds of civilians in addition to the military contingent."

"Are you saying there is nowhere?"

"I am saying, Miss Flynn, that beggars cannot be choosers."

She felt a sudden flush of anger. "And we are little more than beggars?"

He did not reply.

"So where would you suggest a beggar should go, Lieutenant Ferguson?"

"Can you sew?"

"I am a very fine embroiderer, if I do say so myself."

He nodded and pointed back across the Residency at the lawn. "You see the road directly across there? On the left is the hospital, on the right is Dr Fayrer's house. Tell him you can sew."

"Thank you—" She was cut off by an explosion somewhere close by. Fear gripped her heart and she could hardly stop herself from shaking. "Is it always like this?"

"Aye," he said. "All the time."

"How can it possibly be borne?"

"What choice have you?"

And with that he strode away.

ix

Barbara woke her mother and assisted her down from the trailer. She seemed none the worse for their ordeal though she complained of a headache and said she was very thirsty. Barbara did not ask what her mother expected bearing in mind she had been drinking the night before, but the thought of saying it gave her considerable satisfaction.

Her mother jumped at every burst of musketry and shell that crashed. Barbara found it possible to put her fear aside to be strong for her mother.

She took her mother's hand and looped it through her arm and they walked towards the lawn. She stopped before they stepped out into the open. The lumps she had noticed the night before were dead livestock. The air was alive with flies.

Gripping her mother's hand more firmly she set off across the grass at a brisk walk.

"Must we go so fast, Barbara?" whined her mother. "I am not well."

"Better a little discomfort, Mother, than to be shot dead by a musket ball."

"What a terrible thing to say to your poor mother." But she did not slow down and, if anything, increased her pace.

A pair of large artillery pieces sat on the road between the hospital and the doctor's house—and a smaller one in his garden. The soldiers manning the guns were preparing to fire and Barbara took refuge in the doorway of a large building.

She watched them adjusting the angle of the barrels and then igniting the fuse. The sound was deafening. She fancied she could see the ball arching across the city. She certainly saw the explosion though it took a few moments for the sound to roll over them.

Before they had a chance to reload she slipped past them and made her way to the front door of Dr Fayrer's house. They were very close to one of the gates in the defensive wall here and the sound of the musket fire was louder. She had no idea which direction most of the shooting was in.

There was a cry of pain behind her and she glanced round. One of the artillerymen was on the floor, very still. She stared.

"Get the doctor, girl!" shouted one of the other men.

It took a moment for her to realise that he meant her. She banged on the door knocker. For a good deal of time there was no response, and she banged again. An unkempt man with unbrushed hair and dirty clothes came to the door. He was not dressed like a servant so she took the chance he was the doctor.

"Dr Fayrer?" she said and pointed at the prone man.

He shook his head. "The doctor's still abed."

"He must be roused."

"He has had barely five hours' sleep."

"And that soldier has been shot."

The man shrugged and disappeared inside. Barbara considered what a rude fellow he was while she waited. She had an idea that perhaps she should go and see whether the soldier might not be in dire need, or whether he was dead. If at either extreme the doctor would not need to come quickly.

But at that moment a tired-looking man in his fifties appeared at the door. He wore clothing looking as creased as she imagined hers must. It made her less self-conscious.

The doctor hurried across to examine the artilleryman and the man who had answered the door reappeared. She thought that if they were to prevail upon the doctor to provide them with a room it would be important to make a good impression.

"Sir," she said to the man at the door, who was lean and lank with heavy eyebrows that made him look quite disagreeable. "Would you mind attending my mother for a short while? I am Miss Flynn."

How quickly the niceties of polite society were abandoned when need pressed. One did not wait to be introduced, one simply got on and did it oneself.

"Charles Cray, at your service," he said.

"We arrived last night and have nothing to our name. Perhaps, if you would not mind…" she could not quite bring herself to beg for food and hoped that he would offer.

"Certainly, Miss Flynn. I will look after your mother. I'm sure we can rustle up a little breakfast though provisions are carefully husbanded."

She gave him a genuinely grateful smile, perhaps he was not as unpleasant as his demeanour suggested, and turned away. The doctor was kneeling over the prone body. She took a deep breath, trying to prepare herself for seeing a potentially ghastly sight, and crossed the grass to the road.

"Hold his shoulders," the doctor ordered the second artilleryman just as Barbara stepped up to them. The doctor glanced at her. "And you, sit on his legs."

There was an urgency and command in his voice that brooked neither disobedience nor even comment. The soldier was laid out flat. His shirt just below his left shoulder was stained wet with blood. The doctor had cut the tunic and shirt away revealing the bruised and broken skin beneath.

She had expected to feel sick but perhaps it was the intensity and import of the situation that drove such weakness from her. She had barely touched a man, save giving her father a goodnight kiss, in her entire life. But she sat on his legs as instructed, though they had not even been introduced. She suppressed a giggle, realising it was completely inappropriate and wondering what had come over her to even think such a thing.

Sitting on someone's legs was uncomfortable. And when the doctor poked around inside the wound with his thick fingers the agony of it caused the man to jerk and twist quite violently. She watched the poor fellow's face. He was clearly attempting not to cry out but every now and then a groan would escape his body. Barbara could almost feel his pain and her heart went out to him.

She sat even more firmly, resting her entire weight to prevent him from causing problems for the doctor.

"Aha, got it," said the doctor, and pulled the musket ball from beneath the skin. The man went limp; she was not sure whether it was from the relief or from having lost consciousness.

She stood up and brushed her skirts without thinking what a pointless activity it was. "And who are you, my dear?" the doctor asked. He studied the musket ball then threw it aside. He pulled out a dirty handkerchief and wiped the blood from his fingers.

"Miss Barbara Flynn, doctor."

"Well, Miss Flynn, that was good work. Half expected you to need smelling salts."

"I believe I thought the same, sir."

He nodded and turned to rummage through his bag.

"Doctor?"

"Miss Flynn?"

"My mother and I are only just arrived last night, and we have nothing. One of the lieutenants suggested that perhaps my sewing talents might be of interest to you. Though I don't quite understand why."

The doctor turned to her and looked her up and down. "Can you read?"

"English and French."

"We do have a couple of French fellows here. Do you speak the language too?"

"I do."

"What about Latin?"

"I am passable."

"You did not faint at the sight of blood?" he pointed at the artilleryman still lying on the ground though his eyes were now open.

She followed his gaze; she looked at the wound. No, she still did not feel as if she was about to faint. "It seems not, doctor."

"And you can sew?"

"If I may be allowed some pride, though it may be a sin, I believe I am really quite skilled."

The doctor took a deep breath. "All right, Miss Flynn. Well, you sew up that wound and we'll see what we can do."

He held out a needle and thread.

x

She had cleaned off as much blood from her fingers as she could on the artilleryman's shirt once she had finished sewing up the hole in his chest. She had barely touched a man in her whole life, and now she had repaired a wound in a soldier's shoulder.

The doctor had gone off back into the house once he was satisfied she could be trusted to complete the task. She followed and did not even knock. She felt quite unlike herself.

She found her way to the drawing room. There were several people already there. They did not offer her any conversation so she sat by the window and looked out.

She was not sure whether she should be angry with Lieutenant Ferguson. On the one hand he had tricked her into becoming an assistant to the doctor—someone to sew up after he had finished his surgeries. But, on the other, she felt a definite satisfaction in helping save the fellow's life. She had never done anything so important in all her life.

The wall shuddered and there was a tumultuous crash from upstairs. She jumped to her feet. The other people in the room continued talking and acted as if nothing had happened. She was not sure that she would ever become so used to the bombardment that a strike against the house she was in would mean nothing.

"I'm Mary Cray."

Barbara looked up. The words had been spoken by one of the other people in the room. She was offering her hand to shake. Barbara got to her feet. "Barbara Flynn. I'm afraid I have not had an opportunity to wash." She held up her still-stained fingers.

"Oh."

"I was helping the doctor."

"Really? Are you a nightingale?"

"No, well, I wasn't. I don't know. I mean I'm not trained—look, I apologise for being blunt but I wonder if there's a chance of something to eat?"

<<>>

By eleven o'clock that morning, Barbara was beginning to feel that perhaps their fortunes were somewhat improved. She and her mother had been given a room to themselves. It was not very big, no more than a box room really, but still it offered privacy. The other female guests had provided some changes of clothes; they needed adjustment but that was fine. And they had eaten. She determined also that Charles was not Mary's husband but her brother-in-law.

Her mother had fallen asleep on the cot that had been erected. Barbara was wearing fresh clothes and, all in all, she was feeling complete as she descended the stairs.

The doctor was waiting at the bottom and checking the time on his pocket watch. He glanced up at her. He did not smile.

"Come along, time for my hospital rounds."

He strode from the house and turned directly towards the hospital across the street. At the corner of the house he paused. The constant musket fire filled the air but it did not seem very intense.

"Dr Fayrer!"

The voice came more to their left, from the direction of the Residency itself. Barbara saw Lieutenant Ferguson hurrying towards them. She also noted a number of live horses and bullocks tearing up such grass as remained in a frenzy. She loved horse-riding but these animals seemed dangerous.

"Dr Fayrer, you must come quickly! Sir Lawrence has been hurt."

The doctor turned and headed towards him with a long stride that Barbara had difficulty in matching.

"Where is he?"

"In his bed."

They went ahead while Barbara had to trot. The heat was already quite fearful and she knew it would not be long before this dress became as unpleasant to wear as the one she had recently removed.

They entered the Residency building and crossed a black and white tiled floor in need of a good clean and polish. Everything was covered in dust.

The building stood at the highest and most commanding point of the city, looking down at the river on the northern side. Unfortunately that made it a clear target for the artillery of the insurgents.

The men, with Barbara in tow, mounted the ornate staircase and headed along what had probably been an elegant passage, before the attacks.

The door to a bedroom stood open. Outside stood a man in a civilian suit and another in uniform sat in a chair. The civilian stared worriedly into the room while the soldier seemed distracted. The doctor indicated she should stay outside the room. He disappeared inside while the lieutenant remained with her.

"I see you found gainful employment, Miss Flynn."

Anger flashed for a moment. She suppressed it. "Thanks to you, Lieutenant."

"And accommodation?"

"My mother and I have a room."

"To yourselves? That is most gratifying."

"Sir Henry? Is that Brigadier-General Lawrence?"

"It is."

She glanced across at the two men on the other side of the corridor. She turned away so that she only faced Lieutenant Ferguson. "May I ask what occurred?"

"Sir Henry is the strength of this fortress, Miss Flynn. He commands the respect of his men and serves them well in his turn. He oversees everything and is most sensitive to the needs of our native forces. He spent the night working and retired to his room this morning—"

"Miss Flynn!"

She gave the lieutenant a quick curtsy and headed into the bedroom. The wall was pierced by a hole so large she could have stepped through it without ducking her head. The ceiling was blown out and the walls scorched.

An explosive shell must have entered the room.

Sir Henry lay on top of the covers in his nightshirt propped up with some pillows. His eyes were closed and his face distorted by pain. The bed was drenched with blood. The doctor gestured for her to come over and placed a large rolled bandage in her hand that more than filled her palm.

"I will hold the wound closed. You must wind the bandage around the leg as tight as you may."

Barbara stared at Sir Henry's thigh. There was a deep gouge the length of the doctor's hand—much bigger than her own—from which blood was seeping. If it were not for the blood she imagined she would see down to the bone. Her head spun as if she were going to faint but she forced herself to concentrate.

"Do you understand, Miss Flynn?" The doctor's words came from a great distance.

She nodded and found the end of the bandage. She pulled a length out from the roll. "Please begin, Dr Fayrer."

He lifted Sir Henry's knee and braced his own against the foot to prevent it slipping down. The patient kept his lips tight shut but could not completely stifle a muffled groan at the pain.

The doctor pressed the broken skin together. Barbara took a deep breath and wrapped the loose end of the bandage over the top of the leg. Holding it in place with her right hand, she wound the roll under his thigh with her left. She had to reach out to find her right hand and stuff the roll into it. Then brought her left round again to take it and so complete the first loop.

"Tighter," said the doctor as she went round a second time. She pulled hard to take up all the slack. Sir Henry groaned again. She held back her desire to apologise and turned the bandage around his thigh again and again working slowly towards the knee, while the doctor moved his hands but kept the wound closed.

The doctor took the end from her and tied it off. "Thank you, Miss Flynn. Send Mr Lawrence in will you?"

Mr Lawrence would be the one in the civilian suit. As she exited the room she noticed that Lieutenant Ferguson had left. She felt somewhat annoyed but had more important matters to attend to. She approached Mr Lawrence boldly and hid her bloody hands behind her back when he stared. "Dr Fayrer says you can go in now."

He did not thank her, nor even acknowledge she had spoken. He simply walked past her. She noticed the other man's face seemed quite pale and his eyes were wandering.

"Are you hurt, sir?" she asked.

"No, indeed, Miss…"

"Flynn." She frowned. His voice too was not quite right. It had a wavering tone she would not expect of a military man. And he was sitting. The words she said next sprang from nowhere. They were far too bold for a proper young lady, and yet they came out without a thought. "Would you mind if I were to examine you for wounds?"

He gave her a smile. "Of course, please."

There was no blood on his legs, arms, chest or abdomen. She went behind him and her hand went to her mouth. There was a tear in his jacket halfway down his back on the left, and a little blood around it. Could he be hurt and not realise?

"Don't move."

He did not reply; he was leaning forward and his eyelids were almost closed. She did not hesitate and went through into the bedroom. The scene was one of tragedy: Sir Henry's son, if such he were, sat on the edge of the bed holding the old man's hand. Sir Henry himself was talking in a low mumble such that Barbara was not entirely sure he was making any sense.

She approached the doctor. "The soldier in the chair outside is injured in his back. He is passing out in his chair."

The doctor nodded and collected his things. He left without a word.

The operation on Lieutenant Wilson, as his name turned out to be, was swift and simple. Having opened a larger hole in the jacket and shirt the doctor discovered a shard of the shell embedded in his back. He withdrew it—the lieutenant yelled with pain—and Barbara sewed up the small opening. The shard was only a little more than an inch long, and very thin.

"Probably didn't pierce the lung," said the doctor. "He'll be right as rain in a day or so."

"And Sir Henry?"

The doctor shook his head.

xi

If the emergency with the poor Brigadier-General had been a shocking introduction to the wounds inflicted by modern weapons, the next few hours were like being thrust time and again into the lower circles of Hell.

She did not falter and was not sick. Though for much of the time she was not sure why the doctor wanted her along. He went from bed to bed, checking on each man, and asking the attending staff whether anything had changed.

He checked the wounds, of course, and asked her to look.

Then he would show her the wounds. The leg ripped off by round shot, or the arm, or both legs. The man wheezing his last as he slowly expired with his rib cage crushed. The musket ball wounds. Torn flesh. The man with his eyes destroyed by a ball that hit him from the side. Alive but blind.

It was an arcade of horrors.

And not just soldiers. On the lower floor where the air was even more fetid, there were the women and children. And the prisoners.

"You keep prisoners here?" she said.

"Oh yes, it helps to keep the hospital safe." The explanation was simple: it had been determined that almost no event passed within the walls of the Residency that was not known to the enemy without. The attack on Sir Henry had probably occurred because they knew exactly where he slept. Apparently it had been suggested that he move occasionally but he refused to do so. They knew the location of his room and had deliberately fired on it to kill him. And they had succeeded; he would not survive.

"Do not breathe a word about his injury. The men adore him and the natives become uncertain when someone they admire is killed. We get more desertions."

They continued the rounds. Disease was also rife with smallpox, cholera and unnameable fevers.

"A soldier asked if I was a nightingale," she said to the doctor when they finally stepped from the hospital into slightly less fetid air.

"Some of them were in the Crimea, as I was myself."

"Was it like this?"

"It was different, always cold and wet," he said. "But the horrors were the same. Miss Nightingale and her nurses were certainly a help and her practices are worth continuing I believe." He smiled. "But as to whether you are a nightingale? You are a good seamstress. You have a good eye for when something is wrong and that is a valuable skill. But you do not have the training."

He took out his pipe and sucked on it, making no attempt to fill it. "But if the soldiers ask if you are a nightingale, it would give them great encouragement if you were to say yes. And if you do not wish to lie, just smile.

"I'll be pleased when we have a proper supply of tobacco. I must ration myself to one pipeful per day," he said. "Now, come, let us return to the house and have some lunch. We must visit the native hospital, if no emergency calls us away."

<<>>

The rationing of supplies was not limited to pipe tobacco. Lunch was a meagre affair but there was some meat.

"I daresay we will become quite thin," said Mary Cray. She was seated next to the unkempt man who had answered the door in the morning, her brother in law, Charles Cray. Also seated at the table were Barbara's mother, now fully recovered, Dr Fayrer and his wife Jeannette.

"Do you think this will go on for very long?" asked Barbara. She noticed a glance between the Fayrers. Jeannette put down her utensils.

"Yes, it will go on for a long time and then the natives inside will revolt and murder us in our beds," said Mrs Cray. Barbara stared at her to see if this was some sort of ill-conceived humour but the woman was not even looking, she simply took another mouthful of her rice.

"Surely not. The ones that remain are loyal."

"Yes, of course they are," said Mrs Fayrer.

Barbara's mother piped up. "I heard that the women and children at Cawnpore were slaughtered after being defiled."

"Mother!"

"Do not 'Mother' me. It's what I heard."

Mrs Cray looked as if she were laughing, her head bobbing up and down over the plate. Another look passed between the Fayrers, and Jeannette got to her feet. She took Mary by the shoulders and encouraged her to stand.

Barbara caught a glimpse of her face, streaked with tears. The two women left the room.

Charles took a drink of whiskey. The niceties of society were quickly lost; he did not hide the fact he drank excessively. "Mary's husband, my brother, Major Cray, was an officer in a native regiment. They revolted and murdered him."

"You see, Mother? You must be careful what you say."

"Well, I don't know. I was only saying what I heard."

The native hospital was situated among the main group of buildings to the south, in the direction from which Barbara and her mother had entered the Residency. The doctor seemed to take no mind of the shells and musketry that echoed through the place.

"The majority of the shells and round shot are fired at the walls and buildings in order to bring them down and effect an entrance," said the doctor. "The injuries people sustain are quite incidental."

"That does not make it any better," she said, and almost apologised for her pert answer.

"No, it does not," he said apparently unconcerned. "It just means it isn't personal."

The native hospital was little different from the one for Europeans. The men might have darker skin but the injuries they sustained were the same and their blood just as red.

While they were there an artilleryman was brought in moaning and screaming. His hand was missing. Though she had only been at the work less than a day she identified the injury as being caused by round shot.

Dr Fayrer examined the wound. The hand had been taken off cleanly and the bleeding was not extensive, which she found surprising. Their religion forbade them taking alcohol even as a means of numbing the pain, and the doctor did no more than suggest it in passing, knowing what the response would be. He had already told her that they had a limited supply of chloroform which they tried to reserve for the most serious cases.

"Do you think there is enough skin to sew it up?"

She was surprised at him asking her. She examined the wound more closely, as best she could in candle and lantern light.

She nodded. "I believe I can, if he can bear the pain of it."

She looked into his brown eyes and he nodded.

xii

"Captain Dashwood died," said the doctor.

"But he was only brought in this morning," said Barbara.

"Everyone is weak from overwork, the demand for constant alertness and the lack of sleep. Besides," he said, "it was cholera."

"There has not been a single day without a funeral," she said.

"I fear it will continue in the same vein."

Barbara removed her apron. Being constantly bloodied had become something she was used to, but washing clothing was difficult. The limited availability of water along with the finite supply of soap meant that one wore one's clothes as long as possible.

The doctor pushed up his glasses and rubbed his eyes.

"It is good that God saw to bring you to me when he did, Miss Flynn."

"Your eyesight is not as it was."

He made a harrumphing sound. "You noticed?"

"My father's eyes are quite weak. You have the same habits."

"I'm sure that new spectacles would do the trick, but they are quite hard to come by in the present circumstance."

She looked out of the window into the dark of the evening. The sky was filled with clouds and the air with the threat of rain. It was terribly close with the heat. The smell of rotting carcasses was, if anything, worse than when she had arrived but the last ten days had taught her much including why: Animals died from lack of food, or being struck by artillery or musket fire and they could not be buried or disposed of within the walls. Instead they needs must be removed outside.

But there were two problems with that: a great many animals had died, and there were not enough men to deal with them. And getting outside was not easy with the enemy at the gates. So they rotted inside the grounds or were simply tossed over the wall to rot just outside which was barely an improvement.

"They are turning the horses out tonight," she said.

"All of them?"

"They are keeping the healthiest fifty, and the bullocks."

"At least they won't have to feed them."

"That's what Lieutenant Ferguson said."

"I see."

<<>>

He met her at the door of the doctor's house. It was completely dark, raining and her eyes could not adjust to such complete night.

"Thank you for assisting, Miss Flynn."

"You need people who are good with horses, do you not?"

"It is best if we have one person to a horse."

"Then lead on."

She barely noticed the musket fire. It never stopped. She could not imagine how many thousands of the enemy must be beyond the walls. So many they could take turns firing at the walls all night and all day. With artillery guns that fired more or less constantly. She was so tired during the night from her exertions that she did not awaken to shells going overhead or their explosions.

It was so dark she did not see in which direction he went.

"Lieutenant, I have lost you already."

"My apologies, would you care to take my arm?" His voice grew louder as he came back. She reached out her hand and her fingers bumped against his chest. She caught her breath—one did not touch another person like that, especially a man.

"You have found me," he said as he caught her gently by the wrist and tucked her arm around his elbow. She felt a little light-headed as she had been on the night they first met. So little time ago. It seemed like a lifetime.

There was a double thump from behind them. She recognised it as their own battery by the Water Gate to the north—near the hospital. The firing from that direction increased, as did the musket fire.

"It is a diversion," said Lieutenant Ferguson out of the darkness. "The enemy will focus their strength on that side while we open the gates and get the horses out."

They walked past a building near the barracks. There were dim lights shining through thin curtains that allowed one to see where one was going. A man in a Lancers' uniform brushed past them. She could smell the rum on him. Perhaps one of the horses being turned out was his.

She watched as he knocked on the door of the house with the veiled windows. A woman's silhouette showed when the door opened and she let him in. The woman glanced up and met Barbara's eyes, then turned away and closed the door.

Barbara shivered. A whorehouse in the Residency? She only knew what happened there in theory and that was quite enough knowledge for her.

"Are you cold?" Ferguson's voice held the barb of sarcasm.

"It is nothing."

"You're not ill?" This time there was genuine concern and it was an understandable one considering the diseases that were abroad among the population.

"No, really. Perhaps someone walked across my grave."

She bit her tongue at such a foolish comment in the current circumstances.

"Well," he said finally. "Let us hope that your grave is a very long way from here."

xiii

The sound of shifting hooves and the heavy breathing of many horses came to her as they approached the gate. It was possible the place smelled of horse as well, but nothing penetrated the fetid odour of rotting flesh.

Each horse had been tied up and hobbled. She had sewn up a gash in a woman's shoulder where a horse, half-crazed with hunger, had attempted to eat her shawl and had taken a bite out of her.

The sooner they got these animals away the better for everyone, including the horses.

There was a press of men and women, both those assigned to the task and volunteers. Perhaps thirty in total. Some of them were Lancers.

"We will send them out in groups, as many as we can control at one time."

Eventually the command came and each person found a horse; Lieutenant Ferguson went through carefully checking to ensure that nobody had missed one. Horses prefer to run in herds and will follow their leader but it was important they were fully controlled until outside and that meant none could be loose.

Barbara found herself with an immature mare. She seemed sweet enough but she nipped. Barbara held her at arm's length as best she could. The light caught on the animal's body and there was a sheen of perspiration across it. The poor thing was terrified.

She understood that feeling only too well. Though she would never admit it she feared going to bed. She would lie on the floor, next to her mother, listening to the constant bombardment—and Mary Cray moaning and weeping in the next room. Sometimes it was difficult to get to sleep. The knowledge that, at any moment, an explosive shell or round shot could come through the wall and kill her dead where she lay; the feeling of being so utterly powerless could barely be endured.

They were moving. She had not heard them removing the barricades from the gate, which was reassuring: if she had not heard it then neither would the enemy.

The barrage from the far side of the compound increased in intensity. The mare became more skittish. Barbara was pressed between the bodies of the horses as they passed through the gate. She found the close contact with a living creature strangely comforting. Then they were beyond the safety of the walls.

They took the horses some twenty yards along the street between the compound walls on one side and the eyeless buildings on the other. If the enemy were lying in wait for them they would be able to do so with complete impunity. They could hide behind the walls of the houses and not be seen.

They removed the bridles from the horses and a couple of soldiers moved between them cutting every hobble. They did not need any word of command. The horses were now free. At the front of the group the leaders gave their horses a slap to get them moving, and the others followed automatically.

Barbara felt strangely naked and vulnerable as the last of the horses passed her, leaving her and the other humans standing in the road. They watched the horses disappear into the dark for a moment and then hurried back inside for the next batch.

The process continued twice more without mishap until there were only half a dozen horses remaining. Most of the volunteers retreated into the dark, satisfied they had done their duty and unwilling to risk a fourth trip into the dragon's mouth.

"You do not have to do another run," said Lieutenant Ferguson in her ear. She jumped and then laughed at herself. He seemed to make a habit of it. He must be very light on his feet despite his size.

"No, I want to."

She felt that if he had been any other man he would have argued, but Lieutenant Ferguson did not. The two of them with four Lancers collected the remaining steeds.

The diversionary cannonade ended and the night was curiously quiet, broken only by the occasional crack of a musket.

Her assigned horse on this occasion was a stallion with impressive musculature. If he had been predisposed to rebel there would have been nothing Barbara could have done to prevent him but he was as docile and obedient as a dog. As she led him away she noticed he had a limp. Her heart went out to the noble beast. He had probably fought in battle, carrying his rider through cannon and musket fire, and was now to be cast out because he could fight no more.

She brushed away a tear and rested her head against his strong face. He nuzzled her neck. There was no movement in the group, and she wondered what was happening.

"He has to lead, Barbara," said Lieutenant Ferguson quietly. "The others will follow."

She gathered up the lead and stepped forward. The other horses made way for the great beast. She led him out into the street and the same distance as before, the others followed behind. She removed his bridle. He had not been hobbled.

He stood there beside her. She gave him a slap. "Go." He shuffled but would not leave.

"You have to go," she whispered in his ear, her voice breaking with the tears she tried to suppress. "Please."

He nuzzled her once more and then limped away. The others fell in behind him.

Barbara broke down in tears. Lieutenant Ferguson put his arm around her, gathered her close and led her back inside the gate.

xiv

If there was one thing that Barbara was grateful for as the next couple of weeks passed, it was that Dr Fayrer was only one of several surgeons. Each regiment had their own regimental assistant surgeon, with Dr Scott superintending.

As a result Dr Fayrer, being a civilian, was not called upon to perform amputations on the wounded soldiers, and they were generally the ones with the worst injuries. The attack on the compound was almost unceasing. The bombardment let up a little at night and if it rained particularly heavily.

But death was a constant companion. Not a day went past without at least one funeral. The enemy had their artillery and sharpshooters placed around their mosques. One of the last instructions of Sir Henry—he had clung to life for another day before succumbing to the dark—was that the religious buildings must not be harmed regardless of the cost.

Barbara did not keep a journal, as many of the ladies did, and each day was much like the next with its own portion of injuries and the need for her to sew up this cut or that stump. She became inured to the sight of the variety of wounds, though it never stopped her feeling sympathy.

The intensity of the firing meant that the soldiers were on duty continually with barely time for any sleep and rest. Even when there was no major attack the rumour of one would often start up, and once more the garrison would go to the alert. She seldom saw Lieutenant Ferguson except from afar.

It was the middle of one night when she was woken by the doctor. They were called to one of the buildings housing a large proportion of the women. Most of the women were without their menfolk: some were married to soldiers; some of their husbands were dead while others had simply been separated by events. The reason for the call-out was that Mrs

Temple's time had come.

When they arrived Mrs Temple had been placed in a room apart, deep in the heart of the building. The place stank of people and poor sanitary conditions. It was hard to say whether the smell was worse than outside but the temperature inside the building was far higher.

With the food being husbanded everyone's allotment was small. Mrs Temple was thin and Barbara doubted she would have the strength for a birth. She smiled at herself: here she was barely eighteen with the thoughts of an old maid. Life in the Residency had that effect. In truth she barely knew what was expected of her; she was no midwife and she hoped Dr Fayrer did not expect that skill from her.

It turned out he did not. There was a midwife among the women. She was an Irish woman with lank black hair by the name of Curran. Barbara wondered from her appearance whether she had gypsy blood. But her hands were clean and she had the air of someone who knew what she was about.

She had Mrs Temple squat, which she did awkwardly, and had Barbara beside her to help support the woman. Dr Fayrer stood by and allowed the midwife to take the lead.

"How many have you had?" Mrs Curran asked.

"Three that lived, two that didn't," said Mrs Temple as if she were discussing the weather. Then she groaned.

"Hold her steady," said Mrs Curran. She turned to the doctor. "This won't take long."

And it didn't. Barbara had heard from her mother tales of births that involved such pain that the mother and baby died. Of babies that refused to emerge and had to be cut out. There was no end to the litany of horrific stories her mother could relate.

But for Mrs Temple, despite her underfed form, the baby was delivered quickly and without too much pain. Mrs Curran caught the babe and the doctor cut the cord.

When the baby cried she could almost feel the exhalation of held breath from the rooms around them. As if all the women had been waiting on the result.

"What will you call him?"

Mrs Temple was now sitting back against the wall recovering her strength. "I don't know, what was your papa's name, nightingale?"

"Edward."

"I've got me an Edward and a George. We'll call him Albert, I suppose."

She took the babe and placed him to her breast which both embarrassed and fascinated Barbara.

Barbara did not know why the people had taken to calling her nightingale—it was not that she did not understand about the Lady with the Lamp, but Brigadier Inglis's wife and her friends, the upper crust, were always about the hospital and comforting the men there. If anyone should be called nightingale, it would be them.

She left with the doctor. "Why did you want me there?"

They paused and took in the state of the firing, in the same way that one might judge the weather before setting out on a walk. It was heavy but not excessive, and the worst of it was from the south. They were going north.

"It is possible for a woman to tear while giving birth."

Barbara gave that some thought. "Oh." Then frowned. "Why would we be made that way?"

The doctor laughed. "When you have left this mortal coil you might want to ask our Maker that very question."

Barbara sighed. "Yes well, I may not have long to wait for an answer."

"And I wanted you to see that life can succeed even in a place such as this."

"Why does the Lord test us in this way?"

"I think you would be better asking the Reverends Harris and Polehampton that question. I'm sure I have no answer."

They arrived back at the doctor's house. She accepted a small nightcap from the doctor, she found it helped her to sleep somewhat, then retired.

Barbara lay in her bed. Mary Cray was awake in the room next to hers. She was crying again.

xv

"Come on!"

Lieutenant Ferguson grabbed her by the wrist. She really should have words with him about that. They were in the trench that had been dug to form a protected walkway through the south eastern part of the Residency grounds across one of the most exposed areas. There had been too many deaths of soldiers and civilians simply walking there.

This corner was occupied by the Gubbins House with the part of the garrison and battery that protected it. Being a trench it collected water and her feet were sodden by the time they came out of it. The Ommaney House was to their left, its upper storey had collapsed last week from a combination of the artillery attack, and then the rain.

He guided her into the house and down into the cellar where a portion of the stone wall had been removed and there was the entrance to a tunnel. This was one of their counter-tunnels against the mining of the enemy. The rebels would drive a tunnel under the British defences and then blow it up, in an effort to bring down the defensive wall.

To date they had either failed, making the tunnel too short, or exploding too far inside the compound without causing any major damage or loss of life. The counter-mines were effective as on several occasions the British tunnels had either intercepted or been driven close to the opposing tunnel and then an explosion brought both down.

However there was the constant risk of tunnel collapse. Barbara dug her heels in and came to a stop.

"What are we doing?" she demanded.

"We intercepted one of their mines and chased them out of it. We're readying charges to collapse it but there was a fight outside and a wall collapsed. I need you to repair Sergeant Westbury so we can get him back inside."

"I'm not a doctor."

"It's a severe cut. He's bleeding and it worsens when we try to move him. You sew it up then we can bring him in."

She hesitated.

"Men are dying, Miss Flynn."

"I see it every day, Lieutenant." She stared defiantly at him, but his need overcame her protest. "Take me to him."

"Keep your head down."

"I don't think they'll be shooting at us down here."

"I mean the roof is quite low."

"Oh."

They made their way through the tunnel. It was rough and ready—if she could be any judge—and bits of the ceiling fell as they went through it. They came out into another tunnel. This one was of much better construction, well-braced and higher though she still had to stoop a little.

The lieutenant stopped and she bumped into him. "Sorry."

"Hush."

They moved forward slowly and in silence. Daylight filtered through from a gap at the end. The sound of musket fire was almost welcome after the quiet of the tunnel. He turned and laid his hand on her bare shoulder, the feel of his skin against hers was surprisingly pleasant. He pointed down with some intensity. *Stay here*. She nodded.

He crept ahead and said something so quiet she could not hear the words. There was a response and he gestured for her to follow then disappeared into the light. She blinked in the sunlight. At least it wasn't raining.

She looked around. They were in what had probably been the cellar of some house but the floor above was gone, and the majority of the walls with it. There were half a dozen other soldiers rolling barrels of powder into the corner opposite preparing to blow up the remainder of the building.

Destroying the buildings that surrounded the Residency walls was a major preoccupation, because it was those buildings that afforded the enemy cover at such close proximity and allowed them to fire into the Residency with such ease. It also provided locations from which to begin the mining operations. Every opportunity that arose to bring down those houses was taken.

Sergeant Westbury lay a short distance from the entrance to the mine. His face was pale with the loss of blood and he was not focusing. Her familiarity with death was such that, at just a glance, she knew there was nothing she could do. She looked at Lieutenant Ferguson; she wanted to tell him there was no hope, but his eyes pleaded with her. She pursed her lips, gathered up her tattered skirts and went over.

"I brought your very own nightingale, Sergeant."

His eyes opened a little and he saw her. "Angel," he croaked.

"Do you have some water for him, Lieutenant?"

She had learnt a trick or two in the weeks with the doctor, such as giving family members things to do to stop them from getting in the way.

The man's thigh was arranged at a strange angle. She guessed his thigh bone must be broken. She lifted his leg and he choked in the agony. She did not stop but ran her hand beneath it. She felt something, a metal spike protruding upwards into his leg.

When a person's leg had been taken by round shot higher than their knee they seldom survived because the blood loss was extreme and rapid. As far as she could tell the only thing preventing him from dying was the spike in his leg which blocked the blood flow. If there were a way to slow the blood flow while repairing the damage, it might be possible to save him, but not here and not now.

She gently placed the leg back in its previous position. He groaned again.

The lieutenant's eyes were imploring. She looked into them and gave her head a slight shake. He hesitated then nodded.

There was a blaze of musket fire from above. One of the soldiers with the powder dropped to the ground without a sound with a hole in his head. Something tugged at Barbara's skirt and she felt a sting in her side.

The soldiers were diving back into the mine. Barbara pulled herself to her feet. Lieutenant Ferguson grabbed her and almost threw her across the space to the entrance. She stumbled and made it inside.

She looked back. The lieutenant was hesitating, looking at the powder.

"Come on!" she cried.

"The fuse hasn't been placed."

There was movement on three sides above them, and the ground around the lieutenant erupted as bullets landed all about him. Barbara saw past him as Sergeant Westbury raised his musket, aiming at the barrels. He would kill them all.

"Now! Come now! Look!" She pointed at the sergeant.

It took Lieutenant Ferguson just a moment to glance back and realise what was happening. As more musket balls fell around him he ran across to the entrance. Barbara was already inside and heading along the passage as fast as she could.

The explosion shook the walls and the ceiling cracked. All the daylight was gone and Barbara stumbled ahead in the dark through air that was thick with dust and smoke. She was thrown forwards, hit a wall and fell to the ground. She no longer knew which way she should be going. The sound of the explosion and collapsing roof fell away. The air felt lifeless and dull, sounds reduced to nothing more than a creaking of the wooden supports.

It was utterly black.

"Lieutenant Ferguson?"

Nothing.

xvi

She didn't cry.

She sat unmoving, her hands gripping a support set into the wall, while the dust settled out of the air. All these weeks she thought she would be shot, or blown apart, or have part of her body ripped away.

Instead she was buried alive. It was almost funny.

Finally she sat down. It was cooler down here than outside. And she was not at risk of being shot. Her mother had always told her to count her blessings—the same mother who never ceased to talk about the bad things in life.

She wondered how long the air would last.

Then she wondered what had happened to Lieutenant Ferguson. It was ridiculous, they had come to know each other quite well and she did not abhor his company, yet they had never been formerly introduced and she had no idea of his Christian name. It was probably something very Scottish.

She had thought him dead before and he had not been. Perhaps he was not dead now. She should check except she had completely lost track of direction. Then again if, as she suspected, both the entrance and the British tunnel had collapsed (it being of much rougher construction) the space could not be very great and she should be able to determine where they came in.

She would have preferred to crawl but her dress made that too difficult. Carefully she climbed to her feet and brushed down her skirts. The right side was sticky, and quite damp. She lifted her fingers and smelled them. Blood. Her side stung like an insect bite. She must have been grazed by a musket ball but it did not appear to be serious.

She licked her fingers; the dust clung to her blood and made it gritty in her mouth. She kept her head down and walked forward slowly, dragging her left hand along the wall as if she were solving a maze. She reached a gap. It seemed to be open at the top but the bottom was filled with debris. She reached inside only to find it blocked further in.

Being wrong about the British tunnel would not have upset her but being correct gave her some slight satisfaction. She pushed on and the ground became steadily rougher and covered in pieces of rock until she could go no further without climbing on to the collapsed material.

She sat down again. So the lieutenant was buried under this.

The silence closed in and the darkness was more complete than anything she had ever experienced. She could hear her breath moving in her throat and lungs; she even thought she could hear her heart beating in her breast.

Then she heard the sound of breathing that she was sure was not her. She held her breath, the sound continued. A slight in and out.

"Lieutenant Ferguson?" Her voice seemed inordinately loud though she was speaking in no more than a whisper.

There was a scraping noise, like a shoe across gravel. Then he coughed.

"Lieutenant Ferguson?"

"Angus." The voice was coming from a little further along the tunnel seemingly from the floor.

"What?"

"My name is Angus."

"Oh."

"We've not been formerly introduced." He broke into another cough.

"Is this really the right time?" Keeping her back to the wall she edged closer to the sound of his voice.

"What's your name?

"Barbara."

"That's a sweet name," he said. "Under the circumstances, would you mind if I used your Christian name?"

She was slightly flustered by his familiarity. "I suppose so. I don't know where you are."

"Not far by the sound of your voice."

She knew there was something wrong since he was able to talk but remained on the floor. "Are your legs trapped?"

"Very good, Miss Flynn—Barbara," he said. "I admit I am a little afraid to pull myself free. The whole thing may give way. Besides…"

She waited for him to continue but he did not. "Besides what, Lieutenant Ferguson?"

"Angus."

"Angus." The word felt strange in her mouth, she felt as if she wanted to practise saying it, so that she would get it right. It seemed to demand a Scottish accent.

"I do not seem able to feel my legs."

"Do you have pins and needles?" she asked in alarm.

"Aye, a while ago, but it's all gone now. Nothing."

"That's a relief."

"Is it?"

She was sure she was just beside him now because his voice was coming from her feet. She moved carefully and crouched down.

"Yes, Lieutenant—"

"Angus."

She sighed. "Yes *Angus*, it is a relief. If you had no sensation it could be that your back was broken. But if you had pins and needles it's probably just gone to sleep because of the pressure."

"You sound like Dr Fayrer."

"Working with him has rubbed off."

"The job was nae so bad then, eh, Barbara?"

"It's a horrible job, Lieu—Angus. And I have not forgiven you."

"It got you a room, food and a change of clothes. Would you rather have been in one of the other houses?"

"I would not have been ashamed to have been with the other women." She knew it was a terrible lie even as she said it. "I was lucky."

"Fair dues, Barbara."

He made a sound between a cough and a groan. Being unable to see his plight made her forget that he was trapped. If the pressure was not removed from his legs there was a good chance he could lose them anyway.

"Do you have matches?"

"I've tried for them, they're in my belt but buried."

"What side?"

"Left. The other side to where you are now."

She took a deep breath and moved forward onto her knees. "Don't be alarmed but I may have to touch you in order to locate them."

There was a pause. "I believe I can tolerate being touched by you, Barbara." He was laughing at her. "I'm sorry but you are so serious but not wanting to offend me and here I am buried to the waist. Honestly, Barbara, if there is anything you can do to free me from this predicament I will be most grateful."

She sighed. "It's a habit I picked up from the doctor. He's always careful not to give offence."

"The regimental surgeons could take lessons. They have no difficulty in causing offence." There was a hitch in his voice and he coughed. He was suffering more than he pretended. In six weeks she had become an expert in the ways of men in pain.

"Try to keep still." She reached out in the dark. Her hand came down on his hair. "I found you."

"How do you know it's me?"

"Don't talk."

Her other hand found his shoulder and with those two reference points she could imagine how he lay face down. She moved closer and felt her way down his back which was covered with small pieces of dirt and debris. She resisted the temptation to brush them away since he might have injuries of which even he was not aware.

"Have a care, Barbara, I am ticklish."

"Be silent, Lieutenant Ferguson. I won't tell you again."

She found the place where his body disappeared beneath the earth and stones that had collapsed on him, just around his waist. She began to move the material off his body. Some she could move easily, but there were larger stones she had to manoeuvre out of the way.

"That feels better already," he said after she dropped a particularly large stone on the ground beside her. Her back ached from the strain of moving it though she did not mention it. Perhaps men and women were not so different.

Embarrassingly she found it necessary to clear the dirt from the area below his waist in order to get at his belt pouches. Neither of them said anything while she did so. She managed to extricate his box of Congreves. She removed one and struck it.

The white flare blinded her but she held it up and blinked quickly in an attempt to take in the scene. After so long in absolute dark, it was like coming out into bright sunshine.

They were in the original, well-constructed, rebel tunnel and the supports all seemed in good order up to the junction with the British counter-mine which had also collapsed.

Before the match burned down she turned to examine Lieutenant Ferguson's situation. It was not as bad as she had feared. There was a considerable mass of material on him but it did not appear to be supporting anything above him. It looked as if she could remove it without causing a further collapse.

She gave him the good news but he did not respond. The match burned her fingers and she was forced to drop it. It spluttered in a small patch of mud and went out.

xvii

Her heart thumped wildly in a moment of panic. Then she calmed herself and resisted the temptation to light another match. They were a resource best husbanded for as long as possible.

She was concerned about the lieutenant and brought her face down close to his until she could feel his warm breath against her cheek. He still lived and his breathing, though a little strained, was strong.

When the match had been burning she had noticed his hair was across his cheek. She brushed it back behind his ear. The skin of her fingers scraped against the bristles of his unshaven face. Touching his skin gave her a strange assurance and comfort.

She realised she had lain her entire palm on his face and reluctantly lifted it free. It was most improper to touch him, especially when he was asleep or unconscious.

She focused on the task of freeing him. Slowly, but steadily, she cleared the bricks, stones, wood and dirt away from his lower body. She had to stoop the entire time and found the work back-breaking, quite literally. Every now and then she would stand up straight and stretch her back.

As she progressed she stepped over him so she had a foot on either side. She was glad her mother could not see her in such a position. She would claim that Barbara had ruined all chances for marriage.

They would have to survive the siege before that even became relevant.

She felt along his legs seeking more debris to move and found a plank that had, perhaps, once supported the ceiling. She could lift it a short way but it would not come free and must have a considerable amount of material weighing it down further into the fall.

She braced herself, making her back straight, and levered the end of the plank upwards. He cried out in pain. She let it slip back and he groaned.

"If you'd not do that I'd be grateful, Barbara."

"At least you can feel your legs."

"If you were testing them, then yes, I can confirm I can feel them. At least the left one."

"I'm sorry…Angus." She still felt awkward saying his name. Such familiarity was reserved for close family.

And lovers.

"I don't know what I can do to get you out." *Or what injuries we might find if we did.*

"Or whether we'd be happy with what we found if we did?"

For one crazy moment she wondered if he could hear her thoughts. But no, it was a sensible question. "Now most of your body is free could you pull yourself forward when I lift the plank?"

"Aye, we can give it a try."

"I'll count, and lift on three."

She adjusted her position and took hold of the end of the plank. She spread her feet so he had plenty of room. She counted to three and applied upward pressure, though not as much as before.

She heard him scrabbling with his hands. Her skirt caught as he moved and she felt it tugging at her waist. Her fingers ached from the tension.

He made a strange groaning sound deep in his throat: a combination of effort and pain. The plank vibrated and tore free from her hands. There was the sound of soil and stones sliding and the crack of wood snapping. She felt a pattering of something on her hair and threw herself backwards as the ceiling collapsed.

She tripped, fell backwards and landed on something soft.

"Ouch!"

"Sorry."

The noise subsided to where all she could hear was creaking wood but it wasn't from above them. Her legs were covered in a layer of dirt but she could move them without difficulty. She rolled off the lieutenant.

"Are you free?" she asked.

"I believe I am, Barbara," he said. "You're my guardian angel."

"If I were I would spirit us out of here." She sighed and sat up. "Let me examine your legs."

"That would be better in some light, don't you think?"

"Of course but we only have matches."

"I believe my hand is resting on a candle."

She fished the matches from her pocket and lit another one. He held up the candle. His hand was shaking and, with some embarrassment, she placed her free hand on his to steady it. Once it was firmly alight she took it from him and placed it on one of the cross beams near the ceiling. It was only a stub but it would last a while. Perhaps there were others.

She looked down at where he sat, leaning against the wall. He was looking up at her. She got embarrassed and had to fight to keep her hands by her waist instead of putting them to her hair.

"I must look a sight."

"Aye, Barbara, you do," he said. "Truth be told you're covered in dirt. I don't think I've seen a lady looking filthier. And your hair is a complete disaster."

She flushed with anger. "Well, you're not looking so well yourself, Lieutenant Ferguson. Frankly your uniform is an utter disgrace."

He smiled. "I like the angry woman better than the coy lady."

She opened her mouth to utter a hot retort, but laughed instead. He joined in but as his body shook he moved his left leg and drew a sharp breath.

"You *are* hurt," she said, immediately serious. "Let me see."

She crouched beside him and pulled up the leg of his trousers. There was extensive bruising already showing around the upper ankle and the calf. Her superficial knowledge of medicine failed her.

"I don't know," she said. "It might just be bruising from the collapse, or it might be broken. I think you should see if you can move your foot, or your toes."

"You'll have to remove the boot."

She said nothing. She did not even look at him, but tackled the laces.

"I don't want to worry you, Barbara," he started.

"If you're going to tell me your feet smell I think I already know that."

"It was nae that," he said. "I think we're about to be saved."

"Why?" she said but then she heard it too: muffled voices and the scrape of tunnelling coming from the Residency side. "Oh, thank God."

"Was my company so unpleasant to you?" He sounded genuinely hurt.

"No, of course not," she said and turned to face him. As she was kneeling by his leg and he was sitting their faces were on the same level. She looked into his eyes just as he was looking into hers.

His right arm came up and touched her cheek. She wondered for a moment if he was going to make a joke about the dirt as he pushed her hair back behind her ear.

He ran his fingers down the back of her ear. She shivered.

"I'm sorry," he said, his voice only a whisper. He let his hand drop. She caught his wrist and brought it back to her face. Her small palm pressed his grimy and calloused palm against her cheek. She closed her eyes at the exotic touch.

She felt his other hand close around her arm and pull. She allowed herself to be drawn towards him. He only brought her half the distance to his face. She opened her eyes and found herself staring directly into his. He had moved to her just as he had brought her to him.

Their lips touched. Both his and hers were dry and dusty. She pulled back slightly and licked her lips to moisten them, and collected bits of dirt on her tongue. He smiled and did the same. She moved forward and pressed her lips against his.

Something inside her moved. It was as if a great weight lifted from her; as if her heart would break and at the same time had become whole. She did not want to move but to spend eternity there, with him. But finally he pulled away and leaned back.

"So sorry, Barbara, you can berate me if you wish. I took advantage."

"No, I—" she broke off, not entirely sure which of the words crowding her mind she should use, and whether any of them made any sense. "You did not take advantage."

There was a crash behind them. They looked round in the same moment and saw a hand poking through the wall.

"I found a space," said a distant voice. "Is anyone alive in there?"

Barbara looked at Lieutenant Ferguson, leaned forward and kissed him on the lips in such a way as to give him no doubt that she did not disapprove. Then she pulled back and got to her feet.

"Yes, two alive. But Lieutenant Ferguson is hurt."

xviii

The fact that Mary Cray was pregnant only dawned on Barbara in the eighth week of the siege. Food was now severely rationed while water was not a problem as long as the torrential rains kept up. Clothes were scarce while the ones they wore were coming to pieces and in need of constant repair. Mary asked her if she had any material she was not using as she had to let her dress out.

The Fayrers' staff seemed perfectly devoted though Mary always flinched when they came close to her when she was not expecting it. Barbara often missed the evening meal as she would be sewing up the wounds caused not only by accident and injury but also by the surgeons' operations. But this evening, in late August, there had been fewer injuries and thus less sewing.

Barbara sat by her mother, across from Mary and the doctor's wife, Jeannette Fayrer.

"The fighting was loud today," said her mother, as adept as usual in choosing the most unpleasant of subjects for discussion.

"On the contrary, Mother," said Barbara. "There has been less firing today. It was quite calm for a change."

"I heard firing."

"There is always firing," said Barbara calmly. "But today it was less."

Mary seemed introspective. She reached for her glass of water and her hand was shaking.

"What if they get in?" she said.

"The men will ensure that won't happen," said Jeannette. "The rebels haven't succeeded yet so there is no reason to suppose they will at all."

Mary was not appeased. "More soldiers die every day. Women are dying. Children," —she placed her hand on her belly— "succumb to disease and injury too. Isn't that right, Barbara?"

"Yes." She couldn't deny it; she saw it every day. A child, a mother, a soldier: none were immune either to the shells or round shot of the enemy's artillery; the shot from their muskets; nor the disease that could strike in the morning and bring death by the evening. The lack of food meant few had the strength to resist.

"You've heard the news," went on Mary, "we won't be relieved for months. We will run out of soldiers if we don't run out of food first."

Again it was true; Brigadier Inglis knew any news he received would leak out eventually so made sure the truth or, at least some of it, was made public—even when it was bad. Their relief column had attempted to approach but had been driven back. The message had come through that they would not receive reinforcements for at least a month.

"We cannot hold out that long," said Barbara's mother.

"We're British, Mother, and we'll do our damnedest to try."

"You know what happened at Cawnpore? They murdered women and children after committing atrocities on them."

"We don't know that as a certainty," said Jeannette, but she said it without conviction. They were sure it was true; there had been independent reports and there were other similar events. It was little wonder someone as nervy as Mary would fear the servants.

Mary cleared her throat and said quite conversationally. "Can your husband get us some poison, Jeannette?" It was as if she had dropped a grenade in the middle of the dining table.

Mary looked from one to the other. "We've all been thinking it. I know."

Barbara could not meet her eye. It was true, even she had looked at the doctor's cabinet of medicines, and wondered which of them would bring her speedily and painlessly to Heaven's gate. But that had been before she had kissed Angus. Not that she had had a chance to even speak with him since.

"He cannot do such a thing," Jeannette said. "He has taken an oath to preserve life. I would not ask him even if I thought it wise—which I do not."

"It is against God's law," said Barbara, though she felt guilty for saying it considering she had seriously entertained it.

"You would be murdering your baby," added her mother.

"What difference would that make?" said Mary hotly. "If I am murdered the babe is dead anyway."

"It is not the baby's soul I would be concerned for," said Jeannette, "it is your own; suicide is a sin and if by doing it you also killed your child that is also murder. You would burn in Hell forever. Is a few hours of painful life worth the eternal damnation of your soul?"

Mary wouldn't be stopped. "What about opium? We could stop ourselves from feeling it."

Jeannette shook her head. "David told me it's all gone."

Barbara watched the conflict of pain in Mary's eyes. The reports of her husband's death were horrific. It was said he had been stabbed many times and left to die of the wounds. If one imagined such a thing being inflicted on oneself, well, it was easy to despair.

"You must live, Mary," said Barbara. "For the sake of the unborn."

Mary seemed to break, as if something inside her snapped, and she wept openly, making no attempt to stem the flow of tears. Jeannette looked embarrassed but Barbara had seen grown men, soldiers, weep from the pain they were forced to endure whether from the enemy's weapons or from the surgeon's saw.

She went to Mary's side, drew her up and took her to her room, helped her to undress and put her to bed. She sat holding her hand until she fell asleep.

<<>>

Barbara went through into her bedroom and closed the door. Some nights she did not bother taking off her clothes before lying down to sleep but she was less tired today and removed them all.

She lay on her side with her head resting on her hand and, just as she did every night, thought about the kiss. And then she thought about the way she had touched him when she was rescuing him from beneath the fall.

Perhaps it had been unnecessary. Perhaps it should never have happened. Perhaps if they had waited just a few minutes the sappers would have come and got him out without the additional collapse.

But perhaps that would have happened anyway and he would have been buried alive.

Two weeks ago, in the Residency building itself, the upper floor had given way, after weeks of bombardment, and six men had been trapped beneath the rubble. Two had been rescued and they could hear at least one of the others for a while but they couldn't reach them without bringing down another collapse on the rescuers. After a while they had stopped calling.

The thought of that happening to Angus made her shiver.

Beyond the walls the crackle of muskets and regular booming of artillery with accompanying crashes and explosions continued.

"Can you get a poison for us?"

She had thought her mother was asleep.

"No, Mother."

"But you are there with the doctors, you could get some."

"Stealing is a sin. And those things that are poisons, even if I knew what would work, are also medicines and we have little enough left for the men who need it."

There was a long silence.

"I am scared, Barbara."

"So am I."

xix

Lieutenant Ferguson pushed open the door to the whorehouse. The overpowering smell of dead animals and people blocked out the usual odours of such a place.

As an official function of the East India Company's military services there was not, officially, a madam or brothel keeper. A supernumerary in the administrative department of the Company was responsible for the running and the health of the women. But it was in the nature of the human creature that one would take charge and that was the case here. Sergeant Brassie, who did frequent the place, had told him to ask for Deirdre.

The other side of the coin was that, as the whorehouse was the Company's responsibility, if there was trouble, it was the Company's responsibility to deal with it. The nature of the problem had not been divulged to him; he had simply been told to resolve the matter.

Raised a good Presbyterian, he was not comfortable with the employment of women for the physical relief of the soldiers. He knew the arguments: better the soldiers went with women who were clean and healthy than those forced to ply their trade in ill-health. But you would never see one of these women at the Sunday services.

"You're new," said a woman's voice from the shadows inside the first room. Everywhere was in shadows. They dared not make a light for fear of being shot at by the enemy, and besides which the supplies of candles and lantern oil were low.

"I am looking for Deirdre."

"A Scottish lad, eh? We don't get many of your sort."

"Madam, I am not here for your services. I am here to speak with Deirdre."

The woman came out of the shadows. She was thin, but that was no surprise since everyone was thin. She appeared to be in her forties and had probably been a handsome woman when she was younger.

"And you're speaking to her."

"I am Lieutenant Ferguson of the 32nd. I was led to believe you have some trouble?"

She nodded. "And you're here to deal with it?"

"I'll do what I can."

"Took your time getting here; they've been like it since yesterday."

"Madam, in case you'd nae noticed, we have been fighting a battle for over two months."

"All right, Lieutenant, keep your hair on," she said. "Follow me."

She led the way deeper into the house and then up to the first floor. She pulled a key from a pocket in her skirt and unlocked a door. She pushed it open and gestured for him to enter.

There was an iron bedstead in the middle of the room, the floor was bare boards and there was not the slightest decoration in the place. With the windows boarded up everything was a drab grey and shadows.

Lying on the bed was a naked man and woman. They were intertwined and did not seem to be moving.

"Are they dead?" he asked.

"No," she said. "You can't see from here." She walked up to the bed, beside their heads, and pointed to where the woman seemed to be nuzzling his neck.

There was a trickle of blood. He realised the woman had bitten into him and every now and then her throat would flex with a swallowing motion.

The woman's neck also bore bruising and teeth marks.

The horror struck him. "They're drinking each other's blood?"

She simply nodded.

"But it must be painful."

She shrugged. "Some people take pleasure in pain, Lieutenant."

He stared back at them and shook his head as if it might dislodge the loathsome thoughts that were infesting his mind.

"Now you know why I kept the door locked."

"I don't understand," he said.

"What do you think would happen if others found out about it?"

He had it in his mind to deny the possibility that others would follow the lead of these two but in his heart he knew she was right.

"Have you tried to separate them?"

"Yeah," she said. "Had a go yesterday after his time was up but they just clung on. Scratched me into the bargain." She held out her arm to prove it, but he could see nothing in the dark. "One thing though, they're both opium eaters."

Most of the opium eaters among the soldiers—European and native—had already deserted out of desperation—and been murdered by the rebels for their trouble.

"We used to let her have a smoke when he came and they'd just lie together," she said. "They ran out eventually, of course, then they used to fuck." He flushed at her crude language. "Then they did this."

Lieutenant Ferguson looked at the naked pair. He was as much a man as any soldier but the sight of the naked woman in this appalling state had no effect on him. Something for which he was grateful.

"So what you gonna do about it?"

"They're not eating anything?"

"Only each other."

"That can't go on for long, can it?" he said. How long could two people survive on each other's blood? And if one of them were to die, would the other eat the dead one?

"If you'd like to stand back, madam, and perhaps lock the door again?" he said. "I'll see what I can do."

He waited while she shut the door and locked it. She dropped the key back into her pocket and leaned against the wall. He crossed his arms and took hold of her wrist in one hand and his in the other, then levered them apart.

The woman screamed and tried to claw at him which was ineffectual as he still held her wrist. The man, however, levered himself up using the lieutenant's grip as a fulcrum and punched his attacker hard in the face.

For someone who must be half-starved and suffering from the lack of opium he was remarkably strong. Lieutenant Ferguson released the woman's wrist and fended off the next blow from the man, then punched him just below the ribs. He collapsed coughing and spitting, straining to breathe in. All interest in attacking the lieutenant was gone.

He rolled on the floor and the woman leapt on him clawing at his neck. The ferocity of her attack shocked Ferguson. He had been prepared for another assault on himself but her animal lust against her former partner was a complete surprise.

He tried to pull her off but she kept turning away and sliding out of his grip. The wound in the man's neck was terrible to see and blood poured from it. He stood no chance of survival after this.

Ferguson watched the woman for a moment; she plunged her teeth into her victim's neck in desperation. The lieutenant took out his revolver and shot her through the head. The man lay still and the blood was no longer pumping from the wound. He was gone too.

No one came at the sound of the gun. It was just another shot in a world where a minute without a weapon firing was more noteworthy than one with.

"You'll have to write a report," said Deidre. "Destroying Company property is frowned on."

"Probably best if we don't mention exactly what went on."

"I expect he shot her then killed himself," said Deidre.

"Yes, that will do."

xx

It was the middle of September, and the siege had been in place for eleven weeks. The number of desertions of native troops and servants increased though there were no murders to go with them. The servants and soldiers who left were simply scared. If the enemy broke through they would be killed along with their masters. Unlike their masters they could blend in once beyond the walls.

Barbara was at the breakfast table with her mother and the doctor's wife. Charles Cray had been shot while crossing the compound the previous week. Barbara found it difficult to mourn; he had not been unpleasant company but there were so many people she had met who had subsequently died the addition of one more carried no power to affect her.

They were waiting on Mary Cray. Breakfast would be little more than some chapattis and a little beef from one of the diminishing reserves of animals they had within the compound.

"Perhaps she has succumbed to the fever that's going round," said Barbara. "I'll go and see."

"Another fever?" said her mother.

Barbara did not care to respond. She placed her napkin on the table'; her hands had always been thin but as she saw her fingers in the morning light they looked almost skeletal. Still the Fayrers had more to eat than the families in the Brigade-Mess that housed the majority of the women and children. And in less cramped quarters, if perhaps a little more exposed to enemy attack.

She climbed the stairs without hurrying; she had little enough energy to expend on behalf of the injured that she was not going to exhaust herself for Mary Cray.

The sound of her knocking blended with the musket fire from outside, making a lethal rhythm. The rebels were busy today, she thought. More injuries would be in need of her particular skills.

There was no answer. She did not knock again but turned the handle and pushed against the door, half-expecting it to be locked. It wasn't.

Her eyes adjusted to the dim light within. The first thing she noticed was the chair overturned on the floor. Then she saw Mary Cray dangling from a *punkha* rope in the ceiling. She almost returned to the dining room but thought perhaps she ought to check the woman was dead—she was in two minds; Mary had been suffering so greatly that to rescue her from the brink of death, if it were possible, might be considered an unkindness. And, after all, Barbara herself had not taken any oath to protect life.

She shook herself. Such unkind thoughts. She picked up the chair and placed it back under Mary's feet in case she had some life remaining. But there was no response. Dr Fayrer had taught her how to check for signs of life after she had finished sewing up a soldier who had died as she mended the tear in his side.

She checked for a pulse in the woman's wrist but found nothing. In this heat a body did not go cold but deteriorated quickly. The flies were already at her mouth and eyes.

Barbara sighed and returned downstairs with her sad news.

<<>>

"Did he touch you?"

Barbara sighed. Clearly the constant death and disease did not satisfy her mother's thirst for the bad in life. "Mother, we have been over this before."

They were heading for the square near the Brigade-Mess from where the food was distributed. They kept close to the walls between the buildings. This was perhaps the safest part of the whole Residency without a clear shot from outside the walls. But that just made it the target for the artillery—if they could not see individuals to shoot at them they fired shells and round shot in the hopes of raining death on them.

"If he touched you, you must marry him."

"Do you really want me to marry a soldier who may be killed at any moment?"

Though, truth be told, she had mixed feelings about that. She had found the kiss to be the most delightful event she had ever experienced. Then again she was no fool; in this place, with all the terrible events going on around them, to have a few moments of peace and the closeness of another human being was bound to contain significance.

"If he touched you and you didn't marry him, you would be worthless."

"Your faith in me and your trust in my word is truly beyond belief, Mother."

"Show some respect, miss."

"Show some to me, Mother."

They were passing the building that housed the official whores for the regiments. It was company policy they should be made available to the soldiers so they were trapped here along with everyone else.

Not that she had any sympathy or comprehension for a woman of that sort—but they too were under siege.

She tried not to look, to keep her eyes forward and focused on their goal but when a soldier emerged from the building she could not help herself.

She glanced sidelong at the man. Her heart felt as if it had been stabbed with an icicle. Lieutenant Angus Ferguson adjusted what remained of his jacket and stepped from the building. Without a glance around him he headed in the direction of the barracks.

"Disgusting," said her mother with an edge of loathing.

The fact that her mother had no idea what Lieutenant Ferguson looked like was the only saving grace in this situation.

"Come along, Mother, otherwise the choice cuts will all be gone."

"Choice cuts? You must be as crazy as Mary Cray."

Crazy to care about a man who would visit a common whore? Though at this moment in time, the idea that he might die of some unpleasant disease seemed almost gratifying.

xxi

"Where?" she demanded of the native boy. He was young, perhaps ten or twelve, and out of breath. He had run into the hospital where the sight of so much pain and blood had been too much, and he simply collapsed.

She had been closest and picked him up—he weighed nothing and his ribs showed clearly under his skin. She carried him into the doorway but not out into the light where they would be prey to a sharpshooter. He revived quickly and she gave him some water.

"You come quick," he said and pointed in the general direction of the western part of the compound, directly past the Residency building—now little more than a ruin. The rebels still shot at it as if levelling it would somehow bring down the walls and the defence.

The firing from that direction was sharp and clearly there was some attack going on, some attempt to breach the walls. It was unlikely to succeed because that wall was covered by the guards at the Gubbins' battery. The enemy tried anyway.

"Wait, I must get my things." She was not entirely sure how she had been promoted from sewing wounds to front line nursing duties but it seemed Dr Fayrer and the other surgeons trusted her to determine what was needed before they arrived. She had acquired a bag with a few useful items. There were almost no medicines left, even if she were qualified to prescribe them, but she had clean bandages along with her needles and thread for sewing.

When she arrived back at the door the boy set off at a run straight across towards the slaughterhouse and animal pens—which were inside a building. The risk in running across the open space was very high but she did not stop to think about it. If it was her time to die, so be it.

So she ran. It was curiously liberating to challenge death like this instead of skulking in the shadows. It took less than a minute to get across, with the sound of fire growing stronger every moment. A round shot hit the ground in front of her and buried itself instead of bouncing. She was showered with mud.

The tops of most buildings had collapsed where they had been struck so often by the artillery. Even as she watched a shell exploded in the building she was heading for. The boy had already reached it and was sheltering by the wall. As she watched he collapsed to the ground as if he were a small tree felled with one blow.

She cried out and increased her speed.

Kneeling beside him she checked him quickly; his head was bleeding but he still breathed. She lifted him once more and made a dash for the slaughterhouse. Musket balls were flying in every direction. Several soldiers had been shot by their own side.

She made it into the relative calm inside the building, though there was what looked like a fresh hole in the wall. She passed the Faraday trailer that had carried them from the outer fortress all those weeks ago. It had been dragged inside and was on its side against a wall. There was a group of men in a clump in the middle of the room. Two of them were crouched beside one lying prone.

"Someone take the boy please," she said loud enough to penetrate the noise of guns and artillery. The wall shook as something struck it. One of the men took him from her. "Lie him down somewhere; he should survive."

She pushed her way through the crowd. For one moment she thought the soldier lying there was Lieutenant Ferguson and she could not account for the sudden pain that drove through her heart. But it wasn't him.

There was a pool of blood on the floor.

"We didn't know what to do," said someone.

The soldier was missing an arm and the blood still seeped from the ragged wound. The bone had been snapped off and protruded from the flesh. The rest of his arm must be somewhere. His open eyes had lost the spark the living soul gave them. He was dead.

"There was nothing you could do," she heard herself saying while there was a thought in her mind that she could not quite grasp. "A wound like this bleeds fast. Unless you can catch it the loss of blood is too quick."

Too quick? That thought nagged her too. There was something she was not thinking of.

She stood up and sighed. The room shook again and a cloud of dust fell from the ceiling. She looked around at the room. There were great slabs of stone with animal carcasses in various states of dismemberment. And flies by the million.

She wondered for a moment how flies would cope with the Faraday effect. Despite all the horrors she had seen the thought of the flies on the meat she would be eating filled her with a disgust that seeing a man with his arm ripped off no longer did. Had she changed so much in such a short time?

The Faraday trailer sat there leaning against the wall. It no longer had its wheels; they had probably been cannibalised for something else.

"Are you all right, miss?"

"Yes, I'm fine, thank you," they looked to her for guidance, nothing but a young girl but in matters of life and death she was their nightingale. "When the attack stops find someone to collect the body. Until then, just—" what was there to say? "—carry on."

She stared at the upended Faraday trailer trying to capture the elusive thought.

"Is the machine broken?"

One of the men looked where she was staring.

"No, miss, not broken but it serves no purpose. And even if it did we have nothing to burn to give it power, and even if we did the rebels would just target the smoke and blow us all to kingdom come."

"Who knows how it works?"

"Not me."

"No, I mean, who is there here who knows how it works? Who can I talk to?"

"I do hope this isn't going to take very long," said the chief surgeon. "We have patients to see to."

He and the rest of them were gathered in the slaughterhouse. Barbara was slightly amused by the irony though she was careful not to show it.

"Yes, sir, I will proceed quickly," she said. "I know we have many problems in dealing with our wounded, not least being disease and their weakness of strength due to the conditions."

Dr Scott glanced around the room, his attention wandering. He had not been in Crimea and, unlike Dr Fayrer, was not used to discussing medicine with women.

"But blood-loss during operations and immediately after injury is one of the problems and I believe I chanced on a way to reduce it."

Dr Scott jumped in. "Sergeant Haines has volunteered to assist in demonstrating this new technique."

The sergeant was lying on the Faraday trailer. She unwrapped his wound, which was barely seeping blood now. The surgeons had gathered round. "I'm afraid I must open up the wound in order to increase the blood flow."

She gave the sergeant a pained and apologetic look, he gave her a wink, then using a blunt spatula she slid it under the flap of skin and lifted it. To his credit the sergeant only took in a sharp breath across his teeth as the blood began to flow.

"Good God, woman. What are you about?" Dr Scott almost shouted at her.

"Please, doctor, bear with me."

She nodded to three natives in the corner. Coming up with a system of operating the electrical generators without a furnace and boiler had been the biggest challenge. Luckily the billy driver and Faraday engineer, Raj Singh, was taken with her idea and had offered his assistance. It was he who had come up with the human-powered pedal system.

The men pedalled, slow at first but they sped up as they got the flywheel in motion. Mr Singh had explained the flywheel evened out the rotation speed so even if the men slowed down the power would keep flowing in a steady stream.

Such details were not relevant; the results were. Even as they watched the blood flow from the sergeant's leg slowed.

Dr Fayrer was smiling; he had been with them at the earlier test and without his assistance she would not have been able to gather them all together. If she herself had asked, they simply would have ignored the request.

"Apart from the obvious physical effect of the Faraday device in reducing blood flow, I think we can say that the overall strain on the body is reduced," said Dr Fayrer. "And the patient is in a far better state of mind as a result."

"But what is the point?" said Dr Scott.

"You carry out your operations within the Faraday device, doctor," said Barbara. "The patient will lose less blood and will be far more likely to survive."

"Our survival rate is excellent."

Dr Fayrer intervened. "With this device we would have a survival rate far in excess of normal military expectations. It would be a credit to your governance."

Dr Scott smiled. "You really think it would work?"

"If it doesn't we have lost nothing."

Dr Scott looked thoughtful and glanced around at his staff. "Let us have the device removed to the hospital and we will test its efficacy." He shook Dr Fayrer by the hand. "Well, the injuries wait for no man, or machine." With his gaggle of assistants in attendance he left.

Barbara felt empty. She had worked hard for this and Dr Scott addressed all his comments to Dr Fayrer.

"What did you expect, Miss Flynn?" said Dr Fayrer as if he could read her mind.

"I don't know."

"The world is barely ready for female nurses; you can't expect them to fall at your feet." He placed his hand on her shoulder and gave a gentle squeeze, and went off to do his rounds.

She sighed and got out her needle and thread to sew up the sergeant's wound while they still pedalled.

xxiii

She refused to see Lieutenant Ferguson when he called to see her. She claimed exhaustion, which was not untrue. There was not enough food and the constant work of patching injuries that might become infected and kill the patient anyway was sufficient to exhaust an angel.

And she was no angel. She had kissed a man who, it turned out, was quite impure, as unlikely as it had seemed. She sat in the dark in her room with her mother breathing quietly beside her and the background noise of musket fire and artillery. The booms, the explosions and, every now and then, the falling of masonry.

It was so normal to their existence that on those nights when the intensity was less (it never stopped) it was so unusual they worried what the enemy could be planning next.

But tonight was a normal night.

And every normal night as she tried to get to sleep despite the aches of her body, the pangs of hunger and the soreness of her gums—scurvy was rife but one did not die of it quickly—despite all this her thoughts always turned to Lieutenant Angus Ferguson.

He was just a commoner and he had common tastes. He was no suitable match for her. Her mother had not ceased to rail at her about the time in the tunnel. It was tiresome, but then her mother was tiresome.

And Lieutenant Ferguson was a man who succumbed to the desires of his body with loose women. She imagined him lying with one of the Company prostitutes, his naked body and the woman naked. And then somehow it was her that was naked and lying with him.

"Wake up, Barbara," said her mother. Daylight filtered around the shutters.

It was Sunday and every week they made their way across to the

Brigade-Mess where the Sunday service was held.

Dr Fayrer's servants had not deserted and seemed quite loyal. Mrs Fayrer and the doctor were always kind to them and treated them with respect, though Barbara's mother did not trust nor like them. It was embarrassing since she seemed quite incapable of keeping her opinions to herself.

The servants had prepared the breakfast as usual, meagre though it was. Before the siege, such a small amount of food would have had her craving more within an hour but now her body was so adapted it would last her until midday, or all day if there were many wounds to be dealt with.

Breakfast was soon over. Dressing for church was a thing of the past; all their clothes were in such a poor state of repair that there was very little choice.

The soldiers were no better; there was not a man in any regiment that now had a complete uniform. Even though "new" clothes became available on a regular basis as the clothes and goods of men who died were sold off. Sometimes luxuries became available, smuggled in from outside by natives who managed to get in and out.

Such things were bought and sold at astonishing prices but as Barbara and her mother had arrived with nothing they could not buy such things. Once there had been brand-new cloth for sale. She could not imagine how it had been brought in, yet there it was. It had been snatched up by some of the more well-to-do ladies.

As for Barbara herself, her one remaining dress—patched with the remains of those that were worn out and torn—remained decent enough. But still dirty. There was no soap to be had and although the clothes were taken to be washed they came back little different from before.

Church was at nine o'clock, before it got too hot. As the year moved into autumn the days had become less hot and the incessant rain had stopped. This was both good and bad. The rain was depressing and made everything damp, but it did provide fresh water. The temperatures had dropped on the average but water was scarcer.

The enemy had managed to drop two dead bodies into a well and the natives would no longer drink water from it. She did not blame them, even though their reason was religious rather than for health. She was grateful that her religion did not require her to stop drinking the water.

At a quarter to nine she set off around the Residency with her mother and Mrs Fayrer. She thought briefly of poor Mary Cray; she had found church to be a comfort while she had lived. But apparently not quite enough of a comfort.

The Brigade-Mess was located along the south wall. It was considerably less dangerous there than it had been because a small force of soldiers had managed to bring down the Johannes house opposite the wall so it was no longer possible for the enemy to fire from close range or open up a mine inside. Apparently Lieutenant Ferguson had led the expedition.

It was a fine morning; the sun had yet to clear the buildings and the sky was blue with pleasant white clouds scudding across it. There was a brisk wind which carried away the worst of the smells. The sound of gunfire was quite distant.

"Oh," said her mother and stopped walking. Her mother often stopped because she did not survive well on such small amounts of food and tired very easily. Barbara paused and turned.

Her mother turned up her face to look Barbara; there was a tear in her eye and she reached out her hand. She mouthed a word that might have been Barbara's name and crumpled to the floor.

Blood matted the back of her head.

Barbara knelt beside her mother. She took her outstretched arm gently and felt for the pulse in her wrist. There was none.

She stood up again and looked around. The world continued to move but she felt strangely still. Mrs Fayrer was looking at her. Barbara looked down at her mother again and then back.

"I don't know what to do," she said.

xxiv

Mrs Fayrer found two men to fetch a stretcher and they carried her mother's body back past the Fayrer house to the hospital. Barbara walked beside them in silence. They had covered her mother's face and it was hard to believe that it was really her beneath the shroud.

They placed her in the morgue along with the other dead bodies. Barbara looked around with a lack of any real curiosity. She had been in here before, of course, but always it had been in that detached way when one of the patients died. As they did so very often.

One part of her was surprised that, after seeing so much death, this should make her react any differently. Why did she not treat this the way she treated all the others: as something unfortunate but of no real meaning?

After all what meaning did it have? An old woman who delighted in the worst possible gossip had died. An old woman who took pleasure in baiting her daughter about things that had not happened.

Except they had.

Barbara pulled the shroud from her mother's face. She still looked hurt and surprised.

"I'm sorry, Mother," she said. "I lied to you."

Of course you did, you're just a whore like the rest of them.

"I only kissed him."

Liar. You put your hands on him.

"I had to to save his life; he was buried."

Your pretty excuses mean nothing. You touched his body.

"Only his legs, mother."

Liar. The thought is the deed.

Had she really wanted to do more? Had she thought about it then?

Or had that come later? She could not even remember.

"All I wanted was someone to hold me."

"That's all we ever want, Miss Flynn."

She jerked her head up and saw Dr Fayrer just inside the door. When she saw him, her tears suddenly began to flow and she sobbed. He threaded his way between the corpses and put his arm around her shoulder.

"At least it was quick," he said. "So Jeannette tells me."

Barbara nodded through the tears.

"They said a prayer for her in church."

"That was kind," she said and felt as if her chest would burst. She was not sad; she was angry. "Why? Why did God do that to me?"

"To you?"

"To her. To us?"

"I used to ask myself that question a hundred times a day, Barbara," he said quietly. "Until I realised that it was not a question that would ever be answered."

"You don't believe all is chaos?"

"No, but I don't think we are capable of seeing the Divine plan. We just deal with its consequences."

"I do not think Dr Scott is able to deal with those consequences."

The chief surgeon was no longer tending the men or carrying out operations. He walked quietly from place to place. He visited and spoke with people though not as a leader but as a man who was broken.

"I think he will recover. Once he stops asking the question."

She cried again and wiped her eyes with the ragged hem of her sleeve. No one carried kerchiefs anymore.

"I didn't know what to do," she said. "She fell down and I didn't know what to do."

She sobbed as the doctor held her quietly.

After a while the tears stopped. She sat up and sniffed.

"Why don't you find your Scottish soldier?"

"No," she said abruptly. "He is not my soldier."

She sneezed. The doctor frowned and put his hand against her brow, then took her wrist and felt her pulse.

"How are you feeling, Miss Flynn?"

"Cold." And she promptly shivered as if to prove the point.

"You have a fever, I think," he said and stood up. "Can you stand?"

She tried but found her legs were not strong enough to lift her. "What's wrong with me?" she croaked, her throat ached.

Dr Fayrer shook his head. "We are beset with fevers we cannot identify, let alone the ones we can." Then he smiled. "But, if you recall, they are seldom fatal."

He helped her to her feet. She leaned against the table where her mother lay. "Now if you'll just excuse the imposition, let me feel under your arms."

One at a time he took an arm and lifted it so she swayed beneath it, while he felt from her forearm down to where her ribs ended. "Good, no swellings. I will help you back to the house. You need to lie down."

"But people need to be sewn up."

"You are an excellent seamstress, Miss Flynn, but we can't have you infecting the patients, can we?"

"No, doctor."

The journey from the hospital to the house, though it was not far, seemed like a dream that lasted a lifetime. And for some of it she imagined he was Lieutenant Ferguson and attempted to kiss him.

Somehow she kept missing.

The next thing that she knew clearly was she was in the room where she and her mother slept. Where was her mother? Oh yes. Dead. Then Jeannette removed her clothing and found a nightshirt for her from somewhere.

Barbara found herself shivering incessantly. "Can't you make it any warmer?"

The doctor's wife laid her in the bed. "Mother won't like me sleeping in her bed."

"She won't mind, Barbara, you're not well."

Then a glass was pressed to her lips and she found she was very thirsty. She drank it all down, lay back and knew no more.

Jeannette Fayrer found her husband outside the door when she left.

"What do you think?" she asked.

"She's young and strong; she should be fine."

"But this came so quickly after losing her mother."

The doctor sighed. "It may be a product of the loss, or perhaps she was already sickening for it. These things strike so quickly."

"And we have no medicine?"

"Little enough," he said. "And what we do have I cannot give to her; we must save it until it is truly needed."

"That is not fair."

"No, my wife, it is not. But that is the way it is."

XXV

She had no idea how much time was passing. Whether it was days or weeks or just hours. Her dreams were feverish and complex. They left her exhausted as if she had been working hard, though she could remember nothing of them except echoes of horror and fear.

Every once in a while there would be someone there and she would be forced to sit up and drink water. Sometimes she would wonder why her mother wasn't there to help her and then she would remember her mother was dead.

She would miss the funeral. Her mother would never forgive her.

There were occasions that whoever was helping her would make her leave the bed and crouch over the pot. She had the idea she should be embarrassed but she was insufficiently connected to the real world for it to have any real meaning.

And always her dreams were filled with the sound of musket fire and artillery booming but she knew those things were in the real world.

Then she woke up and it was dark.

She knew she was awake. Her head ached. Her mother was dead and her heart ached. Then she slipped into real sleep.

When she awoke the second time there was light filtering through the shutters. There was a full glass of water and a chapatti on the dresser beside the bed. She sat up carefully, her head still hurt but not as badly as it had before. She could still feel the fevered dreams in the back of her mind and the thought of them made her shiver.

She sipped the water and chewed on the chapatti, forcing each thoroughly chewed mouthful past her dry throat.

She slept more and awoke to someone entering her room.

"You're awake then?" said Jeannette.

"Yes." Her mouth formed the word but no sound came forth. She concentrated and repeated it successfully, then added. "How long?"

"Three days."

"It seemed longer."

"That's the way of fevers."

There was a knock at the door, it opened and Lieutenant Ferguson stood there. His face was a picture of concern.

"The lieutenant has been at our door every moment he could get away," said Mrs Fayrer. "And possibly more often than he should."

Barbara wanted to send him away but she neither felt strong enough to complain nor did she want to be unpleasant in front of Jeannette.

"Well," said Mrs Fayrer. "It is, of course, most improper, but I'm afraid I shall have to leave you two alone. I have things to do."

She refilled the empty glass and supplied another chapatti. Barbara was concerned that someone must be going without because this was far more than she should get in a single day. On the other hand she was very hungry so she said nothing.

Jeannette paused at the door. "Do not tire her, lieutenant. She has been very ill."

Barbara wondered what she was about, since not only did she leave them alone but shut the door on them. It was about that moment she realised she was only wearing the same nightshirt she had been put in three days ago. She felt very self-conscious but any attempt to cover herself would only draw his attention. Not that he was a stranger to a woman's body, apparently.

"I am sorry about your mother," he said.

"Thank you."

Without being asked he took the hard-backed chair near the bed and sat on it the wrong way around so his legs were splayed either side. His uniform was not faring well. He had a shirt and trousers that were not regulation. Around his waist was a leather belt with his revolver, and he had a bandolier across his shoulder. He looked like a pirate.

"Have I done something to offend you, Miss Flynn?"

"Me? Not at all."

"I think you have been avoiding me."

"I assure you I was genuinely sick."

"Of course," he said. "I did not mean that. Before, after the tunnel."

"Before and after the tunnel? Really, lieutenant, your command of

English is quite deplorable."

"Aye. It is and you are deliberately misinterpreting me. What is it I have done that you find so offensive you cannae bring yourself to speak with me plainly?"

She shrank back at his onslaught.

"Were you offended by the kiss? Because, if I recall correctly, it was you that kissed me."

"You joined in."

"It would have been impolite not to do so."

She felt flustered, his hurt seemed so genuine. Why did he not see that his common behaviour with women was offensive? Why did he not feel guilt?

"So, were you offended by the kiss?" he said.

"No."

"No? You were not offended?"

"I…was not offended by the kiss."

"Well, that is at least a mercy." He straightened and leaned back a little. "So perhaps you'd care to explain what it is I have done to warrant your poor opinion of me?"

The words built up inside her until she could no longer hold them back. "I saw you coming out of the whorehouse!"

He paused. "Oh, really?" She was quite outraged when he had the effrontery to laugh. Then he stopped and his face became very serious.

"Miss Flynn. I assure you I have never availed myself of the services offered by the Company's camp-followers," then he added as an after-thought. "Or any others not on the Company payroll come to that."

"But I saw you!"

He nodded. "Yes, Miss Flynn, there was one occasion when I was ordered to deal with a situation inside the brothel. One that was quite strange and delicate. I may explain to you when we are out of this place. But, Miss Flynn," he looked at her earnestly with the eyes that she could not help but trust, "neither on that occasion, nor on any other, have I bedded a woman in a brothel."

She looked at him. She knew she should have been shocked at the nature of his words but she did not believe she still possessed the faculty.

His demeanour changed from assertiveness to uncertainty. "Do ye believe me?"

The feeling she had severely wronged him was very strong within her.

She could have simply said "yes" but something inside demanded she be more convincing than mere words. With an effort she got herself on to her feet. She was weak but strong enough for this.

On her bare feet she shuffled across to where he sat. He looked like he was about to stand which would have ruined everything; he was too tall. "Stay," she said and placed her hand on his shoulder, then she leaned forward, tilted her head to one side and kissed him firmly.

When she lost her balance and fell forwards, he caught her.

xxvi

In a trice he had lifted her into his arms and in a stride brought her to the bed.

She was very conscious of the fact that only a single thin layer of material separated them. Her entire right side was pressed against his body and though he had more in the way of clothing than she did, it was still not much. His skin, where they touched, seemed hot.

She almost regretted it when he placed her on the bed. The sheet was partly under her. He hooked his arm under her legs to lift her and untucked the sheet. He drew it over her but it only covered her to her waist.

She was watching his face and did not fail to notice his gaze flicking across her body.

"Thank you, lieutenant."

He turned and for one moment she thought he would leave but instead he brought the chair to the bed and sat beside her. But he said nothing.

"I hope you were not offended by my forwardness," she said.

He shook his head. "Not at all, Miss Flynn."

"I thought we were past that stage…Angus." She was astounded by her own daring. She felt light-headed but that could be because she had barely recovered from her illness. In fact this could still be a dream.

"Barbara." His voice was almost a growl, the sound emerging from his throat.

"Is this real?"

He frowned. "What?"

"I have been feverish, I don't even know if this is real."

"Were you happy in your fever dreams?"

"Not really."

He hesitated. "Are ye happy now?"

She thought, right at this moment, he most resembled a puppy hoping to be petted and not berated. So she smiled and saw the relief wash across his face.

"Yes, I am happy."

"Me too."

He reached down and took her hand. His fingers brushed against her leg and she felt a tingle run down to her toes. She desperately wanted him to touch her more. She guided his hand, pulled it up to her cheek and pressed it there. His touch was wonderful but she was scared.

"You have to tell me if I do something wrong," she said.

"I don't understand."

She looked away in embarrassment and focused on the rough skin of his fingers against her cheek. "I do not know what happens between a man and a woman." Her face flushed. "I want you to be patient with me. I want you to tell me if I do something wrong. I don't know what is—" she searched for the right word and did not find it. "—proper."

He smiled gently. "I do not think anything we are doing at present could possibly be considered proper, Barbara."

"You know what I mean," she said with an awkward defiance, and glanced up into his face.

"Will you allow me a confession?"

She nodded, worried again.

"While I may have heard more about what happens between a man and a woman—I am a soldier after all and they do like to boast—I am as experienced as you."

As experienced? "Oh."

"So, you must tell me if I behave," he smiled, "improperly."

She nodded and wondered how they would proceed if neither of them knew how to behave or what was to be done. She believed she understood the final act, but there must be more to it. Surely there was?

A shell landed outside the window and exploded.

"An eighteen pounder," she said. He nodded.

"Carnal relations outside of wedlock is a sin," she said.

"Yes."

"Perhaps that was God's warning."

"And the rest of the shells for the past two months?"

"Warning someone else?" Suddenly she could not stop herself from laughing. It terrified her, as if she were not in control, but laugh was all that she could do. Angus stared at her for a moment then his face broke first into a smile and then he too was laughing.

Her fear subsided and the laughter continued, bolstered by his. She gripped his hand tightly as if she would never let it go. They both shook as the laughter took them. Then she was crying. And he enfolded her in his arms as she sobbed.

Finally the emotion subsided. The laughter and the tears had drained away from them both. She pressed against his chest, their arms about each other, his shirt still wet from her tears. Her heart felt lighter somehow, though she was now quite exhausted.

She brought her hand round between them and gently pushed him. His arms fell away and she sat back. She saw that he too had been crying but his eyes were brighter now. She reached out and brushed the wetness from his cheeks then brought her damp fingers to her lips and tasted the salt from his tears.

"I believe I love you, Lieutenant Angus Ferguson."

"Miss Barbara Flynn, the feeling is quite mutual."

"You love me?"

"I love you."

She thought she ought to cry at his words but that was not the emotion that gripped her. Instead it was elation and a delight that threatened to explode from her if only it could find expression in the mundane world.

"I am happy," she said.

He pressed his lips against hers and she felt a surge of something within her. She flung her arms around him and dug her fingers into his flesh, not caring whether it caused him pain. In his turn he pulled her roughly into him, her back bent quite awkwardly but she did not care. All she felt was a strange animal fire that wanted to consume her and him in its heat.

His nails scratched down her back and she felt a thrill instead of pain. All she wanted to do was to succumb to it. She broke off the kiss and pulled him closer, burying her head into his shoulder as if trying to make him one with her. She nipped his neck with her teeth and he growled. She did it again.

His hands were under her nightshirt and ran skin to skin along her spine. One hand came between them and pressed against her breast. She pushed back, crushing him to her.

The dinner gong rang.

They stopped moving. She did not want to let him go; she wanted whatever it was that she could feel within her, desperate to explode.

The gong rang again.

She was so close to him she could feel him swallow.

"We must go down to dinner."

"I cannot. I am not dressed." His hand was still on her breast but unmoving. The fire within damped down a little. She pulled away from him. His hand fell away and the nightshirt covered her again. She missed his touch. Her legs were completely naked and visible.

"Would you mind averting your eyes?" she asked.

"Of course."

He stood, perhaps a little awkwardly, and turned his back on her with his arms crossed. She adjusted the nightshirt so that it was as decent as it could be and carefully got under the sheet.

"You can turn round now."

He did so. Until now the sin of lust had been a mere concept, but she recognised it in his eyes and it made her glad.

He bent over and kissed her. Without another word he left, closing the door behind him.

She discovered a smile on her lips. Imagining it was him she placed her palm on her breast and fell asleep.

xxvii

"Major General Havelock and his men will be here within days," said Lieutenant Ferguson as he ate the food he had brought with him. He was seated opposite Barbara at the table with Dr and Mrs Fayrer on either side.

The rations had been cut even further, though the doctor and Barbara had a larger allowance than most, since their services directly assisted in the defence of the Residency. It would have been inappropriate to have forced the Fayrers to provide food for their guest—though they would not have complained—but bringing one's own food when coming to dinner was the new etiquette.

The lieutenant visited whenever he could but he and Barbara had not had an opportunity to be alone together for several weeks. His duty was to the protection of the Residency and she understood.

So they were reduced to making cow's eyes across the dinner table.

"So it's nearly over?" said Mrs Fayrer.

Lieutenant Ferguson hesitated. "I would not want to raise unfounded hopes."

They all nodded at this. Apart from the false alarms of enemy attack that happened with such regularity it was difficult to take any notice of them anymore, they had been promised relief more than once in the past and it had not been forthcoming. It always had a bad effect on morale. There would always be a spate of desertions when expected relief failed to arrive.

Many officers were reduced to looking after their own concerns, without a single servant. Lieutenant Ferguson had never had one so it was no great hardship to him.

"How much longer can we hold out?" asked Barbara.

"Brigadier Inglis says we have food for at least another month."

Barbara nodded. She barely remembered what a full plate of food looked like. Or the last time she had eaten a green vegetable, or some fruit. There was no tea remaining anywhere in the Residency, nor liquor of any sort. They were forced into a state of complete temperance. So when they had finished eating they sipped their water as if it were an after-dinner drink and played a hand of rummy before the lieutenant made his farewells.

Neither the doctor nor Mrs Fayrer ever protested when Barbara showed the lieutenant to the door and, oddly, not even a servant appeared during the minutes they were alone.

They stood together in the dark. Arms wrapped around one another. They kissed and she would feel his lean frame beneath the tattered remains of his uniform.

"Must you go?" she always said.

"I must."

But this night he did not pull himself away from her but held her even closer.

"What's wrong?"

"I must lead a party outside the walls."

She did not protest. He was a soldier; he had to follow his orders. "How long will it take?"

"A few hours."

"What time will you be leaving?"

"Midnight."

"Will you come to see me as soon as you are able?"

"Of course."

She held him closer and rested her head against his chest. "I will wait on your return."

She felt him pulling away and let him go.

<<>>

The evening barrage started up shortly after the evening prayers for the Muslims. All the races and creeds of India had turned against the British together. She did not truly understand why, though Angus had said it was because the British believed they were always right.

It did not explain why they felt they had to slaughter women and children. Her mother was no longer around to tell the horror stories, and embellish them. Mary Cray no longer wept and cried out in the night. But Barbara would have forgiven them all their foibles and fears to have them back among the living.

There was no oil for lamps among the civilians and candles were fetching prices that left one aghast. She and Mrs Fayrer shared a single candle in the drawing room. The weather was turning cold at night now, which was a mercy since they needs must keep the windows barred.

Sometimes she would read until her eyes were too tired, generally not very long, by the light of a single candle. But this night she could not focus on the words at all. She ached with the lack of food and the possibility that the one person she loved in the world would never return.

"Will you join me for a little walk?" said Mrs Fayrer closing her book.

"Thank you," said Barbara.

Mrs Fayrer stood up and straightened her dress. "I know Brigadier Inglis frowns on it but if he had his way we would remain cooped up all day and night."

"His wife disobeys him on occasion," said Barbara almost conspiratorially.

"Gossip, Barbara?"

Although Mrs Fayrer was smiling Barbara was mortified. "I am becoming my mother."

"I don't think it's that bad," said Mrs Fayrer. "After all, I believe she does indeed stretch her legs from time to time, and in daylight too."

They went out by the side door, away from the nearest wall. It was something of a miracle the doctor's house was still standing as most of the isolated buildings, like the Residency and the church, were in ruins.

The sky was clear and there was no moon. The night air was cool with a breeze that brought in fresh air and reduced the smell. If it had not been for the constant firing it could almost have passed for pleasant.

They heard the boom of artillery and moments later the thud of round shot somewhere. It wasn't close.

Barbara looked out across the city. Here and there were injudicious lights. Just as they could not afford to show any lights for fear the enemy might shoot at them, so the rebels were at risk from the British guns.

"Do you love Lieutenant Ferguson, Barbara?"

"I believe I do."

"Is that wise?"

Barbara gave a quiet, desperate laugh. "No, it is not wise but I do not believe it can be helped."

"Your father still lives?"

"As far as I know. He was in the south at the Fortress."

"Would he approve?"

Barbara hesitated. She thought about her father, austere and disapproving, he did not like very many things. Except money. If Angus had money her father would have been happy with the match. If Angus had been an impoverished lordling at least that would have been something to capitalise on.

But he was neither.

"No, he would not approve."

"And you are not yet twenty-one."

"Not for some time." Barbara turned towards the shadow that was Jeannette Fayrer. "You are not going to forbid me from seeing him?"

"My dear, I have neither the right nor the inclination to do so," she said. "We risk death at every turn in this place. Tempt fate by coming out for a promenade. You spend your day sewing up the wounds of men who may die in a minute or the next day." She took a deep breath. "Whether I approve or not, I would not deny you the happiness that you have found."

Happiness? Every day was a torture, not knowing whether she would see him again. It was not simply that he might die, but she might too. Or worse either could be maimed and waste away. Or like poor Corporal Winthrop, the bullet that lodged in his skull took away his reason and though he would not die, he was as helpless as a babe. What if it happened to Angus? Or her? And yet.

"Yes, I am happy in spite of it all."

"And that, my dear," said Mrs Fayrer, "is the greatest gift there is."

xxviii

Morning came but Lieutenant Ferguson did not.

She felt as if she had barely slept. She dressed in the remnants that hid neither her arms nor her ankles. But almost every woman was in a similar state and it was not as if the men had the energy to look.

She ate breakfast in silence. Jeannette did not try to engage her in conversation for which she was grateful. Barbara left the house and found the doctor already hard at work. A new batch of fresh wounds had found their way into the hospital. She froze when she recognised Sergeant Brassie nursing a wound to his arm that needed sewing up. Angus had not said he was going with the sergeant but why would he not?

Fear of what she might learn kept her rooted to the spot. The sergeant waved his arm at her, then flinched at the pain he caused himself. She went over to him and unwrapped the makeshift bandage. It was a bullet wound that had cut through the surface. It was deep and the edges were rough but the ball itself had not lodged in his muscle.

She laid out her sewing kit.

From inside the hospital were muted screams of agony along with the whirring of the pedal-driven generator. An amputation was in progress with the Faraday. She desperately wanted to jump up and find out whether it was Angus, but the terror that it might be him kept her sitting where she was.

She glanced in the direction of the operating area.

"One of me lads," said Brassie helpfully nodding in the direction of the screams. "Got his foot taken off by shot on the way back."

"Is…" she started to ask the question to which she feared the answer.

"You're Miss Flynn, ain't ya?"

She nodded. Brassie looked serious. She found her fingers were trembling and put down the needle.

"Is…" she didn't know how to ask. How could you enquire whether the man you loved was alive or dead?

"I'll tell ya, Miss. I don't know what 'appened to the lieutenant. Not rightly."

"He's not dead?" Her relief was like a sob.

"Like I'm trying to say, I don't know whether he's alive, dead, captured or free."

"What happened?"

Brassie looked her in the eye then glanced around. "Looks like you got plenty of business here, Miss Flynn. Not just me."

"I'm sorry. Yes, of course." She busied herself once more and threaded the needle. "This is going to hurt."

Brassie smiled grimly. "Best get on wiv it then."

It was two hours later when Barbara finished with the new batch. She was sure the number of injuries was lessening though whether that was because the enemy were shooting less or they simply had fewer soldiers to shoot she did not know.

She stepped out of the hospital and found Brassie sitting with his back against the wall. He was smoking a pipe.

"Where did you get tobacco?" she demanded.

"Found it on our little excursion."

"Are you going to sell it?" She knew that Dr Fayrer was missing his pipe; of an evening he could be seen with it clamped between his teeth drawing on it vainly.

"Well, I could buy me commission on the proceeds if I did," he said. "But no. I'd rather enjoy it myself, and enjoy watching others watching me."

She waited. She wanted to scream at him. She wanted to beat his head against the wall. Anything if he would just tell her what had happened. It seemed that he took pleasure in her discomfort, a more despicable version of her mother. And he seemed in no hurry at all.

"Please tell me what happened." she said at last. "Where is he?"

"What will you give me?"

"What?" She shouted hotly. "I could just ask someone else."

"No one else saw what happened."

She felt all her strength leave her. "What do you want?"

"A kiss."

"Why?" she said. "Why would you torture me? Why would you put a price on the truth like that?"

"I have my reasons, Miss Flynn," he replied. "You think your lieutenant is such a decent and up-standing soldier. He's not as perfect as you think he is."

"And me giving you a kiss would make that better?"

He shrugged. "It's my price."

She stared at him. It was just a kiss, and a blackmailed one at that. It had no meaning and no value. "Very well, let us find somewhere more secluded."

"Right here and right now, or my lips are sealed forever."

"But…" she looked around. There were the artillerymen at their guns and various others. No one looked at them. Abruptly she leaned down and kissed him on the cheek, the sort of peck you would expect from a maiden aunt.

"I want a bit more than that."

"I don't know what you mean."

He looked at her slyly. "I'm a soldier, Miss Flynn, in this god-forsaken hole. I could die tomorrow. I could die in a minute, or in an hour. Would you withhold your favour from me, someone who's protecting your life?"

She looked around again. Still no one was paying attention. Musket fire spattered randomly through the Residency. She remembered how her mother had fallen.

"All right, Sergeant Brassie, but you will need to stand up."

He grinned and pushed himself up. He was not much taller than she was. It was not that the sergeant was an ugly man, or he was old, but the way he leered at her made her stomach turn. When Angus looked at her the desire in his eyes was wholesome, but with Brassie it was corrupt.

She took a step backwards, and shook her head, almost involuntarily.

"Don't be afraid." He held out his hand to her.

"I'm not afraid of you, Sergeant Brassie," she said hotly. "I am disgusted by you. I do not know what women you are used to dealing with but I assure you I will not succumb to your blackmail."

His eyes grew dark and his face suffused with red. "You slut." His hand flew and struck her across the cheek. The force of it made her stagger and she brought her hand to her cheek. But she stood up straight.

"Sergeant Brassie, you are an insult to your sex."

She turned on her heel and headed back into the hospital.

"Then he'll die and you've let him."

Just inside the hospital door she shrank into the shadows and pressed her back against the stone. She brushed away the tears with fierce and abrupt strokes of her fingers.

"What have I done?" she whispered.

Condemned Angus to death. He would die because she would not kiss another man. Was that not the height of arrogance? Did she value her own honour above the life of the man she loved? No. Angus would likely as not kill Brassie for his presumption. She was sure Angus himself would rather die than she succumb to Brassie's pressure.

And where would he have stopped? The thought made her shiver. If he was a man to force a woman's favour in such a way, what made her think that he would even keep his word? Was he not more likely to lead her down the path into deeper debauchery? She had seen his eyes uncloaked.

But what of Angus?

Brassie had said that she had condemned him to death. A small piece of truth that slipped out in his fury at being denied. Angus was alive somewhere outside the Residency. In her heart she had always known that to be true. He was safe but unable to get back.

Was he captured by the enemy? No, if that were true there would be no point in saying she had condemned him. There would be no way in which anyone could rescue him. So he was alive outside the walls, not a prisoner but unable to get back. Either because he was injured or because he was trapped in some way—just as they had been in the tunnel. So she must find him and rescue him.

She wiped away the remainder of her tears. She felt different. There was a focus in her mind she had never before experienced. Her every action and thought was now guided by a single purpose.

The first step was clear: she must find out where they went on their expedition. There were other men from the 32nd in the hospital; she would make enquiries. The men would respond to their nightingale.

So she went about the beds finding the men of the 32nd who had also come in that morning. She had sewn up more than one of them. It did not prove difficult to discover the story.

To the east the rebels had constructed a new battery for a set of thirty-two pounder guns. It was not yet operational but elephants had been spotted bringing in the guns and it would not be long before the battery would be knocking down the walls of the Brigade-Mess and the buildings around it. The safest part of the Residency would cease to be that and their defence would be seriously impaired.

As a proven man of action, and a member of the official regiment for Lucknow, Lieutenant Ferguson had volunteered to lead the attack to spike the guns at least, preferably to destroy them.

The outward journey had been managed in secret and they had launched themselves upon the guns. They had killed many of the rebels and spiked the guns. They had set the charges to destroy the battery and Lieutenant Ferguson had sent all the men heading home with their wounded while he and Brassie prepared to light the fuses.

The enemy had been pouring into the area once alerted to the intrusion. The charges had not gone off and only Brassie had returned, saying they had withdrawn because of enemy fire without lighting the fuses but he had lost the lieutenant.

Barbara's blood boiled when Brassie's part of the story was related because she knew it to be a lie. But there was nothing she could say, because it would be her word against the sergeant and in their eyes she was a mere emotional woman. They did not advertise their relationship, since it was unofficial, but it was not a secret.

She had one of the men point out the location of the new battery. It was visible from the hospital which meant they were all at risk. Thankfully they still held rebel prisoners in the hospital which kept it relatively free from bombardment. Although the occasional stray shell still came through.

The new battery was about a quarter of a mile away. She fetched a bible and used a blank page to sketch a map, using the mosques as landmarks. The mosques were the only buildings that remained untouched since Brigadier Inglis continued to enforce Sir Henry Lawrence's policy of respect.

Despite the complexity of the debris-covered city streets she felt sure she could reach the place. But how would she find Angus? She did not know; she must trust to Providence.

She gathered up some supplies that might help if he was injured. Candle and matches she purloined from the doctor's house.

She spent a portion of the afternoon working, sewing up injuries and operation wounds. She found it hard to concentrate and still had the final problem to deal with. How would she escape the Residency walls themselves?

Evening drew in and, as the light faded into night, it became impossible to sew so, as usual, she left her post and headed back to the house for the meagre meal that awaited her.

"I was sorry to hear about your lieutenant, Barbara."

Mrs Fayrer's words jerked Barbara from the depths of her hopelessness. She could think of no way to get beyond the walls.

"Yes, thank you."

Barbara tried not to catch her eye.

"I would have thought you would be more upset."

"I am very upset."

"Not a single tear and here you are eating."

"We were not that close."

"Ha!" said Jeannette. "Now that is a terrible lie. Seldom have I seen two young people so besotted with one another. And under these conditions too."

"He's alive." The words burst from Barbara like a musket shot.

Jeannette looked at her. "Are you given to delusions?"

"I know he is. His sergeant told me as much."

"Brassie? I dislike him. Are you sure he's not just lying to you? He strikes me as the type."

Barbara poured out the whole story barely pausing for a breath, ending finally with "Do you believe me?"

Jeannette Fayrer looked at her. "And he truly demanded favours of you to tell you where the lieutenant is?"

"He did."

The doctor's wife studied Barbara's face, though she seemed to be lost in her own thoughts as she did so.

"Help me."

Jeannette sighed. "My husband, not to mention the other surgeons, would be very displeased if I were to lose their best nightingale." Barbara opened her mouth to plead her case again, but Jeannette held up her hand.

"Please allow me to finish. However if I do not help you I imagine you will make the attempt anyway and will be more likely to fail."

Barbara held her tongue though the excitement was threatening to burst from her.

"We will see what can be done."

"Thank you!" Barbara leapt from her chair and threw her arms around the woman.

"So, you had better be successful otherwise you put me in a very difficult position."

"I will succeed," said Barbara. "God willing."

xxx

The first choice of costume Mrs Fayrer had offered was as a Muslim woman dressed head to foot in black and face veiled, the clothing taken from a woman recently deceased. This would have worked if Barbara could have spoken the language but it would have been very hampering and the first challenge would have undone her.

Instead Barbara suggested wearing men's clothing would be more practical so Jeannette rustled up a pair of the doctor's trousers and a dark waistcoat to go with it. They dirtied up a shirt and rubbed mud into her exposed skin. She would attempt stealth rather than deceit.

At the last moment Jeannette had come to her and handed her a lady's pistol. "It has two shots," she said. "I was keeping it in case of the worst." Barbara took it gingerly and thanked her.

There was an old Hindu woman who had been in and out of the Residency more than once carrying messages. She was found and asked to take Barbara out with her. She refused at first since she had no desire to put the girl at risk. Even an offer of money did not seem to tempt her, though she got paid well enough to carry messages.

When the real reason for the escape was given she acquiesced—but took the money as well, with no promise to return her charge. She would only take her beyond the enemy lines just outside the walls. To get past the Residency garrison Barbara wore the Muslim garb over her other gear, with her bag tied to the trouser belt.

And so it happened. When they passed through the main gate in the south, there was some argument over Barbara's presence. It was claimed she was a mute and was being sent back to her family in the south where there was no trouble.

This seemed to work and within minutes they were outside the walls.

Barbara stayed close behind the old woman who ducked through a crumbling building. They climbed down into some old entrenchments which wound through the collapsed city. Barbara heard the soldiers talking, though she could not understand them. They sounded no different from the British soldiers when they were on duty.

They passed through the lines and the woman came to a halt. She pointed towards the east along what had once been an alleyway between buildings. Once it would have been alive with people, now it was just shadowy corpses with black, empty windows.

The woman took Barbara's hand, squeezed it and said something unintelligible, but if she were to make a guess Barbara would have said it was a blessing.

Then she was alone. The dark form that was the woman merged with the other shadows and was gone.

Everything here was strange and different. The sound of firing had a different echo. The artillery boomed and was lost quickly instead of rolling across the landscape. The smell of rotting flesh was far less here.

She stripped off the Muslim robes and put them to one side. She opened her bag and checked, by touch, that everything was there. She took a deep breath and set off in the direction indicated, stumbling over broken rocks and trying to make as little noise as possible.

The dead city was a maze. She did not know how to navigate by the stars. All she had was the memory of the map she had drawn for herself. But she could see nothing save broken walls.

She needed to get up high to see where she was. There was a building that seemed in better condition than the others. She was not foolish enough to go inside. It was common enough for damaged buildings inside the Residency to simply collapse; there was no reason it should be different here.

Instead she climbed a stairway exposed when the rest of the building had fallen. She noted that trousers did indeed provide much easier movement.

She reached the second floor and heard voices from above her. She silently cursed herself. If this building would give her a better view then, of course, it would give the enemy a better view as well. She knew it was reckless but she went ahead anyway.

The voices appeared to be coming from the building's roof. She stayed one level down and worked her way around to the eastern side. There was a fire burning in the distance and it highlighted the walls and corners of the mosques. She had come almost half the way to the new battery and, from her elevated position, she could even see the gun barrels.

She looked back the way she had come. The Residency grounds looked open and vulnerable. The buildings were like broken toys. She took a deep, calming breath. She was alone with the enemy around her and no idea where to search for Angus. This was the height of foolishness, and a fatal foolishness at that.

Perhaps she should have tried to present her case to Brigadier Inglis— but then Jeannette Fayrer knew Selina Inglis and even she had not suggested that course of action. She had encouraged her to come out here into the very jaws of death. A sudden fear came over Barbara: what if Jeannette were jealous of her relationship with the doctor—they were together so much of the time when he was away from his wife.

But that did not make any sense; Barbara was in love with Angus. That was why she was here. No, Jeannette would not think such a thing. But the doubt tainted her thinking like a dirty stain. She gave herself a shake and focused on her task. She would aim for the battery and see what she could discover.

There was a flash, and a sound that boomed like thunder rolled across the city. One of the thirty-two pounders in the battery had spoken. The shell shrieked overhead. She turned her head to watch. There was no explosion inside the Residency and moments later there was an eruption on the far side that silhouetted the buildings.

A cheer went up from above her. They were ranging the guns. Even if the expedition of the previous night had successfully spiked the guns, that work had been undone at least with one of the artillery weapons.

Six of the guns from the Residency fired one after the other in retaliation. Their shells and round shot exploded around the new battery.

She looked at the rising smoke and devastation. This turn of events had both good and bad points. On the one hand the enemy troops would withdraw from around the battery for fear of being hit, and the attack helped to show her the way. On the other, the area being bombarded was precisely where she intended to search. And where Angus was most likely to be.

She climbed down as another round of fire came out of the Residency. What the enemy did not realise was that the British had barely enough crew to man the six guns currently firing—they moved round between the gun emplacements. And the number of trained men shrank all the time.

She spent the next half hour climbing through the broken remains of houses, trying to keep out of sight while staying on course towards the worst of the bombardment. The one thing they did not lack in the Residency was powder and munitions.

A round shell crashed through a wall to her right and she barely jumped clear of the falling stones and debris. She swore to herself that when the siege was lifted she would go home to England and stay there. But, she reminded herself, if she married Angus she would have to go wherever he was stationed.

She was exhausted. They had been on limited rations for so long that her body was unable to keep up with her desires. There had been no further fire from the thirty-two pounder. Perhaps they were just testing it. The bombardment from the Residency reduced to the occasional pot-shot. They had no way of knowing whether they had succeeded in disabling the guns.

She found a sheltered spot and sat down to regain her breath. Away from the Residency, between the artillery shots, the constant musket fire was reduced to a distant pattering. She had not known such quiet for months.

Which is when she heard the humming of a Scottish air.

xxxi

Barbara's heart leapt with joy. She jumped to her feet and turned her head trying to locate the source of the humming. It was further in towards the battery. She moved forward making the best speed she could over the rough terrain.

She slipped on a stone and her foot sent a smaller one skittering across the ground. The humming stopped. She knew he could not be far. She looked around and strained her ears for any sign of the enemy. All seemed quiet.

"Do not stop, my love," she said quietly, hoping beyond hope he was close enough to hear her.

There was a long silence and then a snatch of a melody line, quieter than before. She judged its direction and headed that way carefully.

Her foot stepped on nothing. She suppressed a cry so it was nothing more than a grating in her throat. She bent the leg that was still on solid ground and fell back against a stone that knocked the wind from her.

"Who?" said a voice in a whisper, yet it echoed.

Barbara had to take a minute to regain her breath and then rolled over to the side of the hole in the ground. There was intense blackness beneath her. "Angus?"

"Am I delirious?"

"Only if we both are."

"I was expecting Sergeant Brassie, is he with you?"

The meaning of that question rekindled her anger but that was a matter for a later time.

"Only me."

A thunderous explosion deafened her as the thirty-two pounder, now very close, spoke again. She covered her ears though it was far too late. The very ground trembled and the edge on which she lay crumbled so she had to force her way back.

She realised that the Residency would start its bombardment again. She needed to understand the problem that faced them. She rummaged in her bag while her ears sang and slowly returned to normal.

A shell from the Residency exploded a short distance away and showered her with dirt and shards of stone. She dug out the matches, lit one as quickly as she could and dropped it into the hole. It did not go out. In its spluttering light she took in the collapsed cellar. It had a mosaic floor on which was a mound of stones. Next to the stones was the highlighted silhouette of Angus, looking up at her. She smiled.

The light went out. He'd been trying to pile up the stones to get height to the hole but lacked the necessary since the gap to be breached was at least six feet. She looked about. The necessary was all about her but how much could she really move?

"Have you got a rope?"

"No."

But there was something that would serve.

"Throw me your trousers," she said quietly.

"They won't be enough."

"Please don't argue." She could see nothing in the pitch black but there were faint sounds of rustling. Interrupted by three shells exploding in quick succession. This time they were slightly further away. The British were ranging better, thank goodness.

Something flew up out of the dark and she snaked out her hand to snatch it from the air. The trousers were caked in dirt. She rolled over, awkwardly unfastened the ones she was wearing and wriggled out of them. She tried not to think of the fact that her bare legs were now exposed to the night, and anyone who happened to look.

She tied one leg from each to the other, made a loop that she could hang on to and dangled it down. The makeshift rescue line went taut as he caught hold of his end. She wondered how she would be able to hold his weight as a couple of round shot crashed and bounced around them.

No choice. With the loop hooked into the crook of her elbow, she pressed the material into the ground with her knee and called for him to climb. From the outset she was terrified. The material slipped immediately and it took all her limited strength to keep hold. As he made his way up he jerked the line and each time she was dragged a little closer to the edge.

Her arms began to shake with the strain and her knee was right on the edge. She would be unable to take another jerk of the line and she would get pulled in. The weight disappeared and her own effort threw her back against the stones behind her.

He must have fallen. But there was no sound. No hitting the ground. No crying out in pain.

"Could you give me a hand?" The words were nonchalant in nature but the voice was strained. His hand snaked up from the blackness. She looped the trousers round a large stone and fed the end into his hand. She pulled hard on the other end and watched as his other hand appeared pulling one after the other.

His head came into view then he got his elbows on to the surface. He let go of the trousers so she did the same and went to his aid. With her help he climbed out and lay panting on the surface.

Two shells exploded together as if celebrating his release.

His head was towards her as she knelt over him. She leaned down and kissed him upside down. It was the sweetest kiss she had ever given or received.

"Are you on your own?"

"Yes."

"No one with you?"

"That is what being on one's own means, Angus."

"Sergeant Brassie?"

She said nothing. He sat up and leaned his back against the stones. He had his boots tied by their laces around his shoulders and his legs, thin but still muscled, were quite visible. Somehow she did not feel embarrassed.

"Did the sergeant not make it back?"

"He made it back."

"He was wounded and the brigadier would not send anyone on so risky a mission."

"He suffered a slight wound."

The Residency set up a barrage now they had got the range. Shot and shells rained down two hundred yards from them. They could no longer talk. Barbara set about untying the trousers. When she stood up to put them on Angus stared at her legs. She didn't care. She wanted him to see her. She wanted him to touch her. She wanted to be naked with him. If only in despite of Brassie.

Once they were dressed the lieutenant set off towards the bombardment, away from the Residency.

"Where are you going?" she demanded, though she already knew the answer. "I did not rescue you to have you throw your life away."

"I have a mission to complete."

"Then I'm coming with you."

"No."

"I came this far to find you, Lieutenant Angus Ferguson, and I will not lose you again."

He nodded and led the way.

xxxii

The two of them were hunkered down behind the solid bank of soil, stone and rocks that had been piled up to protect the big guns. The attack from the Residency had ceased once more, though if it started up they would most certainly be blown to bits. The whole area was pitted with impacts and craters.

Angus put his mouth close to her ear. "With luck the munitions we set up have not been moved. We just need to run a new fuse."

His warm breath tickled her. And she had the strange notion that she would like him to lick her ear. This rapidly led to other thoughts of a similar nature involving other parts of her body, which she pushed away—not because they were unwelcome, only that they were completely out of place.

She nodded instead.

"Stay with me but at a distance. Keep an eye out for trouble."

He moved past her along the edge of the raised bank to the wall of the building at the side. She let him go about twenty paces and then followed.

She couldn't see precisely what he was doing in the dark but he went inside one of the building husks. She remembered her duty and found a large piece of wall to hide behind that allowed her a good view of the area.

The battery for the thirty-two pounders had been placed at one end of a road. To her right, behind the fortification and just visible against the stars, was the skeletal wreck of a municipal building. There were similar ruins on either side of the road flanking it, one of which Angus had entered.

The road itself was lined up directly with the Residency for some distance and any buildings that might once have obscured the view were now flattened. The battery had a clear line of sight.

She jumped at some shouting in Hindi from behind the battery. She tensed and put her hand inside her bag seeking for the little gun Jeannette had given her. The voices did not come closer or seem very angry. They were just shouting to one another.

There was a sound from behind her and the shadowy shape of Angus emerged into the air silhouetted by a flickering of light from inside the building. The tiny light was outshone by a brighter light from behind the battery ramparts. She saw Angus slam his hands over his ears. Realising the danger she did the same as a flash, as bright as day, and a thunderous report exploded across them.

She was struck by a wave of pressure that knocked her to the ground. Having their ears covered may have prevented damage but it left hers ringing along with a terrific pounding in her head.

Angus shook his head in an effort to clear it. The fuse gave them about two minutes to get clear, and the firing of the gun had probably lost them a quarter of that already. It was not that they were in danger from the explosion itself but who knew how many buildings would come down around them once the first started to fall?

He looked at Barbara, once more a shadow in the dark. For a moment, during the flash, he had seen her in her tattered men's clothing, her skin filthy with dirt, covered in dust and debris with her hands over her ears and her face screwed up. He could not think of anyone he would rather see.

It was amazing to think she had made it through our lines and theirs, that she had reached this far, that she had managed to find him. She was a unique woman and he loved her with all his heart. If only they could escape this horror alive.

They had to move.

He dropped his hands, though he could still hear nothing but a whistle in his ears. He caught her by the elbow. She jumped but relaxed when she realised it was him. He gestured to her to follow and they headed off, threading their way along the road.

He was not too concerned about being seen while they were close to the battery since the rebels would already have taken cover expecting the retaliatory bombardment from the Residency. It was only as they approached the front line they would have to take more care.

It was so dark he almost ran into the figure standing in the road. His hand went to his side for his revolver then he realised it wasn't one of the enemy, but a soldier from the Residency in his tattered apology for a uniform.

He stepped back and studied the man and then smiled. "Brassie!" He could hear himself saying the word, his ears must be clearing.

"She found you." The words were fuzzy but understandable.

"Good to see you!" said the lieutenant. He stepped forward to embrace the man. But Brassie stepped back and kept clear which was the moment Angus realised the man held his revolver in his hand.

"I can't believe she found you."

Ferguson was no fool but he had been more than a day without food, though there had been water in the hole. It took him a few moments to go from the realisation that Brassie was here, and that he knew Barbara was here, to the fact that Brassie must have failed to report that his lieutenant was alive. But that he had told Barbara.

Which did not make any sense at all.

"Why couldn't you have just died a hero?" said Brassie. "That would have made it so much easier."

Angus stared at the gun pointed straight at his belly. Did Brassie mean to kill him? Yes, of course he did. He had not reported that Angus was trapped. And he had failed to carry through the mission. He was a coward and now he was going to be a murderer to protect his reputation.

Behind him, the artillery flashed from the Residency. Perhaps they would all die. He glanced at Barbara; she was not as close to him as he thought she would be, but off to the right. She was clasping her bag to her breast. She was probably scared.

Brassie raised the gun.

"Do I get to say any last words?"

"No."

The distant thunder of the Residency artillery rolled across the city. Shells shrieked overheard and exploded behind them. For a moment Brassie was lit up; Angus could see him squinting against the brilliant light. Angus threw himself to the side. A gun shot went off and in the moment of silence that followed there was a tremendous eruption from behind them as the charges set by Angus's squad the previous night went off.

Angus moved again, this time throwing himself at Brassie and grabbing his gun hand. Brassie resisted for a moment. His eyes focused on Angus's face, so close they were almost touching.

"Fucking bitch," said Brassie. His eyes unfocused and he crumpled to the ground, leaving the gun in Angus's hand. The flames from the explosion behind them grew. Angus glanced across at Barbara. She had a gun in her hand pointing at Brassie on the ground.

There was a creaking behind them, then a roar as the mined building decided it could no longer remain standing. It came down in a cloud of dust and buried the thirty-two pounders under tons of masonry. The wall beside them wavered.

"Come on!" Angus cried, throwing all caution to the wind. More shells were shooting overhead and drowning out all other sounds. Angus took her by the arms and gave her a little shake. "We must go."

She nodded and together they headed towards the Residency.

xxxiii

Dawn had not yet made a mark on the horizon when Lieutenant Ferguson met the challenge of the guards on the gate. Barbara knew she should be exhausted but energy still coursed through her. She had rescued Angus and killed a man—albeit one who deserved no better for his cowardice, betrayal and depraved desires.

The gate guards did not question them after Angus told them he would be reporting to the brigadier in regard to the successful completion of his mission, even if it was twenty-four hours late.

Perhaps they assumed Barbara was another soldier. They could hardly expect to recognise her as a woman in her disguise with her hair tied up. Angus did prevail upon them to give him some food and drink which he ate as they walked.

Angus escorted her to the Fayrers' house. At the door and looking back they could see the remains of their handiwork still burning. There was the occasional explosion as another barrel of powder ignited.

In the shadow of the doorway they stood facing one another almost touching. She reached out her hand and caught his. She felt the grime on his hands along with crumbs of unleavened bread. She lifted his fingers up and pressed his palm against her cheek. She kissed his fingers feeling the hunger that had slumbered deep within her since that evening so many weeks before.

His free arm reached around her and pulled her in. She pressed her body against him. Their lips met and she closed her eyes. All she wanted was to touch him, as if her life depended upon it. The hunger was like an animal inside her tearing to get out, fighting to control her movements, to make her do things she desired and feared to do.

He broke off the kiss and trailed his lips across her cheek to her ear. He nibbled the lobe which made her shiver. Then she felt his tongue tracing the contours. The beast within tore free of the bonds she had around it. She thrust her arms under his shirt and felt the muscles and the bones of his back, she scratched her nails down his spine—not knowing why she did it, not caring if it caused him pain.

He groaned. She froze. Fearing she had done something wrong. "Don't," he said into her ear. She pulled her hands away, "stop. Don't stop."

She was faint with desire and tore her nails across his back again. His hands pulled the shirt she wore from the belt and his hands explored her back, her spine, her waist. One hand tried to delve beneath the belt but it was too tight. She felt disappointment. She wanted to feel his hands everywhere.

Then he stopped. His hands ceased to move on her back. He withdrew his tongue from her ear leaving it damp and cold. "I should go," he said.

He tore himself from her. She clung to him like a drowning woman. "No."

"I cannot…"

"Cannot?"

"Must not."

She paused. He was being honourable. He was being the good, kind and gentle man she loved. They were not wed and he would not bed her.

The realisation burst like an artillery shell. She wanted to bed him. She did not care that they were not married, she wanted him. Though the prospect of it scared her—along with the image of her disapproving mother tutting and wagging her finger at her wanton daughter.

She allowed him to step away from her but took a firm grasp of his arm.

"I want you to stay with me," she said.

"I will always be with you, my love," he said. "I promise."

"And I you, my sweet Angus, but," she paused. The words she wanted to say—that the panting creature within her wanted her to say—were there in her mind, she only had to make them real. "But, Angus, I did not mean that."

"What did you mean?" They both spoke in whispers but she could hear the strain of desire in his words. The animal resided within him as well.

She moved close to him once more, placed her hand at the back of his neck and drew his head down. She touched his lips with hers. The lightest, gentlest pressure that might not have been a kiss at all yet she gave it such meaning that even the blind would have seen it. She became one with passion inside her.

"I will not be parted from you," she said so quietly it was barely more than a breath. "I would have you in my bed this night, my love."

When he embraced her again she knew she had won.

In tales of romance the journey to the bed chamber is always performed with the utmost ease and grace. Reality is different. Angus and Barbara crept through the house pausing at every creaking floorboard. They inched up the stairs keeping their weight to the edges to reduce possible sounds.

She led the way but his hands never left her. He touched her shoulder or her back, as she began to climb to the next floor his hand slipped to her waist and then to her posterior. If she had been wearing her skirts she would not have felt it but in trousers, with only her drawers beneath, his touch was like a branding iron. It made her desire strain to run free.

The snores of Dr Fayrer and snuffles of his wife floated through the air. At least they seemed sound asleep. Barbara and Angus crept into her bedroom and pushed the door shut.

It was quiet. Even the bombardment seemed to be holding its breath. Dawn's first light filtered through the window shutters and she could see his face; see how dirty and unkempt he had become. She must look the same. She did not care.

She was breathing deeply in anticipation, as if she had been running hard. Simultaneously they reached out to one another, not to embrace but to unbutton their partner's shirt. They got in each other's way.

"Perhaps we should undress ourselves," he said. The thought terrified her. And excited her. She nodded.

"Let us take turns," she said. "I will go first."

"Very well, Miss Flynn," he said in a way that suggested he thought she would be naked before him. She unbuttoned the waistcoat, let it fall to the floor and smiled demurely. A look of disappointment shot across his face. She looked at him expectantly.

He took off his shirt. He was less grimy beneath it. And woefully thin, but they all were, and she had seen plenty of men's chests in the hospital. She had lost count of the number she had sewn up. His bare chest and arms were attractive but they were no revelation.

It was her turn again. She took off her poor worn out shoes. "Shoes and socks count as one," she added.

"You are making the rules?" he said.

"Who has the most to lose from this encounter, Lieutenant Ferguson?"

He bowed his head in acknowledgement and took off his boots. It took a while and he had no socks. She felt as if she had lost interest.

"Your turn, Miss Flynn."

She weighed up the options. Shirt or trousers. Her chest was of considerably more interest than his. However drawers were separate items, one for each leg. Not joined in the middle, but they were baggy and the shirt was too long and would hide her nether regions.

So, to his surprise, she unbuckled the belt and let the trousers fall. The drawers covered them down to just below her knees. Her legs were no longer plump and soft. The bones stood out clearly. She sighed and found that lust seemed to have wandered far from the room. She wondered if it would return because now all that remained was the fear.

If her lust had gone, it seemed his had not. His eyes were glued to her legs. Surely they were not that different from a man's?

She was about to find out. She stared with a kind of fascinated horror as he unbuckled his belt and undid the buttons. She castigated herself. She had sewn up plenty of legs as well. And stumps of legs. She had not only seen them, she had touched them. Including all the way up the thigh. Three months ago she had been completely ignorant of the anatomy of the male sex. Now she was quite well acquainted with it.

He had pantaloons though they were in a disgraceful state. It did not concern her; she knew her drawers were much the same. Perhaps the suggestion of undressing themselves had been a good one.

The time had come for her to remove the shirt. She felt herself redden in embarrassment but the game had gone too far to be stopped now. She felt the creature within begin to stir, now that she was reminded of the reason they were alone in this room. She unbuttoned it carefully, perhaps teasingly. She turned away from him, as she pulled open the front and let it drop from her shoulders.

She heard the in-rush of his breath as her bare back was revealed to him. She held her arms across her chest and turned back. The animal and the fear were fighting for control within her. She pushed them both down and forced her arms to her sides.

He stared at her breasts. Then realised what he was doing and, with an effort, raised his eyes to her face. "You are beautiful," growled the beast within him.

He fumbled with his pantaloons and pushed them down and stepped free of them, in her direction. She took a step back. It was her turn to stare.

In the growing light his manhood was erect and fearfully large. Her fear was gaining in strength.

Her mother had said that when the monster came out in a man there was nothing a woman could do but succumb to it, to weather the storm and weep afterwards. She had not said that a woman could also be possessed, but Barbara had wanted this. She still wanted this.

She looked up into his eyes. "I'm scared."

He held out his arms to her and took another step towards her. She lifted her hand. "No. Stay."

She held his eyes and found the tie for the drawers; she undid it and slipped the waistband over her hips. They fell to the floor in a dirty white pool. She stepped out of them and came into his arms. She closed her eyes and felt what she had desired. His skin against her skin. Bare flesh pressed together.

He held her. Squeezed her close but did not move. Though she could feel his hot member pressing against her she wanted to feel all of him. The animal inside her woke up, stood and shook itself.

He took half a step back and to the side, with one hand behind her shoulder he slipped the other under her legs and lifted her from the ground. She clung to him as he carried her to the bed and laid her down on it, the wrong way around. He lay down beside her on his side, leaning up on his elbow.

Gently he traced his free hand across her stomach. He scratched his nails across her breasts making her shiver with pleasure. He leaned across and kissed her on the lips. She responded while his hand explored her flesh. The fear subsided.

He seemed to understand what she wanted, despite his claim he had never been with a woman. His wandering hand pressed her breasts in turn. She wanted to touch him but did not know what to do. She recalled what had happened at the door. Her right arm was under him so she reached round and dug her fingers into his back. His response was to squeeze her breast harder which she found pleasing. She felt a little more confident.

She brought her left hand up and covered his right. She squeezed his fingers to make him squeeze her again. He obliged and moved his mouth to her ear again. She scratched circles in his back, her arm was too tightly pinned to do more, but he made appreciative growls.

She was breathing heavily and he was panting into her ear. The animal was fully awake now and guiding her movements once again.

She loved what he was doing to her ear but felt too passive. She wriggled her arm out from beneath him and turned on her side so they were face to face. His eyes were wide open and she looked into them. The lust was in him, just as it was in her. This was what her mother had warned her against. And Barbara understood: if only one of them felt it the result would be terrible. But if the beast was prowling in both it could only be good.

Daring herself, she wriggled closer to him so she could get her left arm all the way round his body. She ruffled his hair. He kissed her. Then she ran her nails down his back and beyond; she gripped his behind and dug in her fingers.

He groaned as she realised that her thigh was also now pressing against his hot male organ. She did not find it at all repulsive. Her eyes flew open when she realised that in the pressure of the kiss he had opened his mouth and opened hers in the process. She could feel the dampness of his mouth within hers. She felt as if she were melting in ecstasy.

He reached back with his free hand and entwined his fingers with hers. She wondered if she were doing something wrong again and almost panicked. But he did not stop kissing her with his open mouth and his chest was pressed against her breasts. It all felt so perfect and so good.

His released her hand and reached round to her back. She shivered with pleasure as he ran his nails down her spine until he reached her behind. His hand was so much bigger than hers he could cup it easily. He applied pressure gently and the warmth she had been feeling between her legs blazed. She had never known anything like it. She made a little noise into his mouth. It made him do it again more forcefully. "More," she said. He obliged.

Then a wanton thought entered her head. His hand was not located in the best place for stoking the fire he had lit in her. She rolled on to her back, pulling away from him abruptly. She saw the look of panic in his face—it made her glad as it meant she was not the only one unsure of what to do. She smiled at him and without looking away from his eyes, took the hand that had moments before been on her behind, opened her thighs, and placed his fingers between them.

She did not release his fingers but taught them how to move—though up until that moment even she had not known. Once he had learnt well enough she released them. He got up on his elbow again and while his fingers practised their lesson, his lips and teeth attacked her breast in a delightful onslaught.

Nothing mattered anymore except the carnal pleasure. He was panting and she had to suppress the noises her body wanted to make so as not to alert anyone in the household as to their activities. Her hand gripped his member—hot and hard and soft—and he thrust with his hips. She knew that he too was in the grip of the beast. She giggled; he was in the grip of two animals.

Something powerful was rising within her. This was something else. It felt like an explosion, like a volcano. Its power was terrifying yet it must be released if only she knew how.

His hand pulled away from between her thighs. His lips released her breast. She felt alone. He got up on his knees; she thought he was going to leave her. She reached out to him. But he moved before she could stop him. He placed himself between her legs.

Oh.

Fear overcame her again. He smiled. "It'll be all right."

I might get with child, she thought. *I might die in childbirth. And we're not married.*

But her body desired him still. The fear was not enough to stop the animal this time. She opened her legs wider; he leaned over her and inched forward. She felt him between her thighs. How could it possibly work?

It was so confusing, the fear and worry on one hand. And her body wanting it, almost pulling him into her in a sensation that felt so perfect. There was a moment of pain and then he was thrusting like a steam engine.

In the strange shock of conflicting sensations there was a cold certainty she had done everything her mother had told her not to do. In the bed her mother had slept in.

Then the fire rekindled. The volcano rushed at her like a giant artillery shell and she exploded. She barely recalled the next few minutes as the ecstasy overwhelmed her. Somewhere in that time Angus too exploded; the thought made her giggle again, in his case it was literal.

Then he stopped.

Just stopped.

He held his weight off her body and then withdrew, sitting back on his heels. He looked at the light coming in through the window.

He looked down at her lying naked with her legs apart. He pulled back and let her roll over. He lay down by her side and put his hand lightly on her arm.

"I'm sorry," he said.

"You shouldn't be," she said.

"I want to marry you."

"With the reverends dead there is no one that can do that for us at present."

He paused then said. "I love you, Barbara."

She rolled over to face him. "You don't have to say that just because of what happened."

"But I do anyway."

She smiled. "You had better go."

He dressed quickly, kissed her and left. She turned round in the bed and got under the sheet. She was very tired and was asleep before she could worry.

xxxiv

She was awoken by Jeannette entering her room with a tray of water and a chapatti. Barbara sat up, pulling the sheet with her as she was still naked. She tucked it in behind her to leave her hands free.

Jeannette placed the tray in her lap.

"What time is it?" Barbara asked.

"Gone noon."

"I should get to work."

Jeannette placed her hand on Barbara's. "I told my husband you're unwell."

"And he didn't want to come and check me?"

"Your monthlies."

"I haven't had that since we got here."

Jeannette nodded. "I believe that's common. The lack of proper food is the main culprit we think."

"You discuss it?"

"My husband is a doctor, Barbara," she said. "We have few secrets from one another and it is in his interests to understand what happens with women as well as men. He often has questions."

"I would be mortified," said Barbara and washed down a mouthful of chapatti with some water.

"That might make the next part embarrassing for you, then."

Barbara tried to look as if she had no idea what Jeannette was talking about.

"Please, my dear," she said. "We are aware you have successfully rescued Lieutenant Ferguson."

"Yes." Barbara smiled. "Yes, I did. I found him and brought him back."

"And he spent some time with you. Here in this very room." Barbara felt her smile turn to stone. "Did he force himself on you?"

"No!" Barbara's vehemence seemed to surprise Jeannette as much as it did Barbara herself. "He did not force himself on me." She lifted her chin defiantly. "If anything I forced myself on him."

Jeannette's eyebrows rose slightly. "Men can be very devious."

"Yes, they can." She thought of Sergeant Brassie. "But not Angus. He was kind and gentle. If I had wanted him to stop he would have. I didn't want him to."

"I see," Jeannette said thoughtfully. "Well, at least it is unlikely you will conceive."

"I do not see that as advantage."

"Oh, you don't? Well, let me ask you this: How will you help mend the wounds of soldiers when they won't let you near them? When they call you a whore and a harlot?"

"It would not come to that."

"You think not? Then you are a silly girl and not the responsible woman I have considered you to be."

Jeannette stood up and took the tray from her. "You may rest today but my husband would like you back tomorrow."

"Of course and," said Barbara, "thank you."

Jeannette paused at the door and turned back to her. "Would you mind if I asked you an extremely personal question?"

Barbara felt a wave of embarrassment sending her complexion red. She did not know what the question would be precisely, but there was no doubt what it would be about. She had taken advantage of the Fayrers' hospitality so did not feel she could deny her. Barbara nodded, wide-eyed in expectation.

"He had carnal knowledge of you."

Barbara nodded again, her flush deepened.

"Did you take pleasure in it?"

"Oh yes!" Barbara gushed. "It was extremely pleasurable."

At her outburst Jeannette looked somewhat put out and pursed her lips. But, after a few moments, a smile replaced her stern face. "In that case, my dear, you are very lucky and would be wise not to lose such a rare fellow."

She looked as if she was going to leave once more and stopped again. "However I must insist you desist from such activities under my roof. The doctor and I also have a reputation to consider."

"I understand."

Then Jeannette did leave, closing the door firmly behind her.

Barbara lay back down in the bed. She found her limbs were still quite sore from the escapades of the previous night. After the weeks of constant work it was good to simply lie there, lulled by the constant musket fire and the booming of artillery.

Then she sat bolt upright. She had shot Sergeant Brassie. Was that not treason? But he had been about to shoot a superior officer. And he was a monster. She was quite sure that if it had been Brassie with whom she had spent the night she would not have found it at all pleasurable. He was a violent man who thought of women as something to be used.

If she had to face a court for killing him she would speak honestly. And God would be her judge.

Her mind drifted to the later events of the night and she smiled at the thought of Angus's naked form. How much better he would look with a few proper meals inside him. She fell asleep as she discovered that a lesser form of the pleasure she had found with Angus could be produced through her own actions and thoughts.

<<>>

She was not arrested for the murder of Sergeant Brassie. The story was told that he had gone out himself to find Lieutenant Ferguson, without orders; that he had located and rescued him from a cellar but that he had died in the escape. He was given military honours.

"Why should his family suffer?" Angus said as they walked together, not touching, from the Brigade-Mess to the post office garrison and back. The safest place for a promenade.

"He was married?"

"His wife and children are back in London. She'll get a widow's pension and perhaps a little extra for his heroic action."

"And I get nothing."

"What would you have me do, Barbara?"

She thought about it. She bore no ill-will against Brassie's family and if this saved them from penury perhaps it was for the best.

"And your reputation would be in tatters if it were known you were rescued by a woman." She knew it was an unkind thing to say but she was tired of the way she was treated simply for being of the weaker sex.

"I think there are many that would admire your actions, both men and women," he replied. "But for most it would be a difficult idea to accept."

"What about you? Is it difficult for you?"

He laughed loudly. "No, my love. Seeing your face in the light of that burning match was the single most perfect moment in all my life."

She smiled.

"I do love you, Barbara."

"And I you, Angus Ferguson."

"If I could marry you tomorrow I would do it."

"I know."

"We could announce our engagement and then, at least, we could hold hands in public."

At which she slid her arm through his and clasped him to her tightly. There was not even a glance from the people they passed.

"I believe our unofficial engagement is already common knowledge."

XXXV

A relief column was promised in early September. That it did not materialise surprised no one. They had had so many false alarms that no one believed any news anymore.

They continued to hold out despite the constant attacks. On one occasion the enemy succeeded in making a breach and getting inside the walls. However they did so in Sikh Square which had been barricaded thoroughly in case of such an eventuality. Every enemy that got inside the walls was shot dead within seconds at no loss of life to the defenders.

It was not Barbara's imagination that the attacks were reducing in intensity. Angus confirmed it. "I believe they have given up thinking they can force an entry and overrun us. They intend to starve us out."

"Which is exactly what will happen if relief does not arrive," she said.

He did not disagree.

The number of new injuries decreased. There were even days with no funerals. Barbara had less sewing up of injuries to do and more free time. Angus, however, did not. Whenever there was a dangerous mission to be undertaken he was always there at the front of the volunteers, whether it was to bring down a house or attack an enemy mine.

She wanted to tell him to stop, to consider how it would be for her if he was killed. But she did not; how could she ask a brave man to contradict his very nature? To negate the thing that made him what she loved? So she held her tongue and suffered whenever he was gone.

The Lucknow garrison received word their relief would arrive but they must hold until mid-October. Another month. Food rations were cut again for the civilians. No one complained; the soldiers were the only ones keeping them from a violent death so they must receive the better allocation.

Angus was not happy that he received more than Barbara and, despite orders to the contrary, kept back food for her. It made her guilty to eat it, but she did anyway. Angus said that a nightingale was as important as a soldier so her strength must be maintained as well.

Scurvy and other diseases became the main killers as the strength of the garrison withered.

The days became a blur. She and Angus did not enjoy any intimacy but, if truth be told, she was glad. She did not have the strength.

On the 5th October fighting increased on the outskirts of the city and they knew their relief was coming in. At midday two officers, wearing uniforms not composed of cast-offs and rags, rode into the Residency and asked to see Brigadier Inglis.

The remainder of their force fought its way up to their fortress and managed to get inside. Major General Havelock lost two-thirds of his force just getting into the city. They brought more weapons and munitions and some additional food but they were just as trapped. The new forces were immediately put on half-rations. Their only benefit was that the new men had not suffered months of deprivation so were stronger.

<<>>

Barbara cried over dinner that evening. She apologised to Jeannette and the doctor for her lack of decorum. They were nothing but sympathetic.

Angus came to her later. The deployment of the newly arrived forces meant that he could have a day off-duty.

They stood in their accustomed spot at the door of the house. In the dark. The weather was turning colder but they had no coats or cloaks.

They said nothing and just held one another. Not even kissing. They had not kissed in weeks.

"I'm sorry to interrupt you," said Jeannette. She emerged from the shadows of the house. "But, my husband and I have discussed the matter and have decided that we wish to rescind our previous stricture in regard to your bedroom, Barbara."

"Oh?"

"Ah, yes. That matter we discussed after the happy return of the lieutenant." Jeannette sounded quite embarrassed. "If you recall."

"Oh, yes I recall the matter in question," said Barbara. It was difficult to know what to say when you have been given permission to fornicate. "Thank you."

"I'll bid you goodnight then."

"Goodnight."

"What was the meaning of that?" said Angus when she had gone.

"It means, my love, should we so wish Dr and Mrs Fayrer have given us permission to use my bedroom for our liaisons."

Angus seemed dumb-struck.

"Do we wish it, Angus?"

"Do you?"

She sighed. "I will be honest, my love. I am exhausted all of the time and I believe my teeth are loosening with the scurvy. I know I am an unsightly skeleton."

"You are beautiful to me."

"Of course I am. Love is blind, Angus," she said. "And I would gladly lie with you to feel your skin against my skin as we did before."

"But?"

"I do not have any strength for…exercise."

"Then, my sweetest love," he said gently. "All we will do is lie."

<<>>

They withdrew upstairs quietly because. Though they had been given permission, it would not be done to flaunt it. Both the permission and the act they were going to perform were far past being acceptable behaviour.

They undressed without the performance they had been through before. Though, this time, it took Barbara a little longer since she was now in women's clothing, no matter how thin and damaged it had become.

They had no light in the room and she squeezed in beside him, feeling his bones more than his muscles. His skin stretched taut as parchment on a frame. He welcomed her into his arms and she rested her head on his bare shoulder, her arm across his chest and curled around him.

Their legs entwined and she pressed herself against the warmth of his body.

"Have a care my love. A gentleman can be quite delicate."

She smiled and dared to speak boldly. "Your ardour is not diminished however?"

He sighed. "It is, I believe, in the nature of the male sex to desire procreation at any time."

"That must be inconvenient."

"Indeed it can be."

"Then perhaps we should only have girl children," she said and yawned. "Boys would clearly be difficult to rear."

"And what of my line?" he said. "Am I to give up my heritage?"

She gave no reply as she had fallen asleep.

xxxvi

The arrangement whereby Lieutenant Angus Ferguson slept in the bedroom with Miss Barbara Flynn continued through the remainder of October and into November. Although, if truth be told, his responsibilities meant he could spend less than one night in five there.

She missed him terribly on the nights he was absent. Instead she hugged the pillow that had come to smell of him. She would breathe his scent and pretend he lay with her.

They always lay together unclothed. There was one night as October turned to November when she felt it was unfair of her to refuse him her body, though she still lacked any desire of her own. It was as if the animal had abandoned her completely.

So, as they lay there, she touched him boldly and encouraged him. He smothered her in kisses and nibbled her ear. She desperately wanted to feel the flaming passion ignite within her but remained cold.

When she opened her legs, though her joints ached, he climbed between them. He kissed her face and prepared to enter her. But he tasted salt on her cheeks and held himself over her but not touching.

"Why have you stopped, my love?" she said, trying to keep her voice calm, lifting her legs to wrap them around his hips.

"You are crying."

"Tears of joy."

"You are a poor liar, wife of my heart."

The grief within her burst through as if it had broached a dam and she sobbed. He disentangled himself and lay beside her once more. He slid his arm under her and rolled her over so he could cradle her in his arms as she cried. And she cried like a child, breathing hard and choking out her sobs.

After a while the intensity of her grief grew less and her breathing became calm.

"I wanted to please you."

He held her tighter. "You always please me."

"A wife's duty, Angus."

"In exchange for a husband's duty."

"Don't be foolish, there is no such thing."

"Between us there is," he said simply. And she began to cry again but this time because she loved him so much.

As one of the few buildings still standing, the post office gave the best view of the advancing forces in the direction of *Alum Bagh*.

Lieutenant Ferguson was impressed by the speed of the advancing troops; while you expected the infantry and especially the horse to be able to advance rapidly, it was not something to be expected of the heavy artillery.

But there was no question. There were guns in excess of eighteen pounders moving and firing at a speed close to that of the infantry. Each one of them appeared to be accompanied by a machine similar to their long-gone billy. The artillery must be mounted on Faraday trailers. The soldier in him immediately perceived the advantage. And the effect on the enemy was demonstration enough: they were withdrawing by the thousand.

A hail of musket fire made him duck behind the battered stone balustrade. A large chunk crumbled and fell. Just because a large portion of the investing forces was moving away did not mean the Residency was safe.

He had been at the briefing given by Major General Havelock and Brigadier Inglis, just lately recovered from one of the unidentifiable fevers that struck for a couple of days and then disappeared. The colonel had honoured the brigadier by giving him the duty of announcing that a force of considerable size was coming to relieve their position.

They had been expected several days hence but had clearly made considerably better time than predicted. The enemy had not had time to regroup and face them, and were retreating in a disordered way.

The occupants of the Residency would be departing in a very short time. Once the move had started he would have no time to speak to Barbara, in fact there was a very good chance they would be split up. He had better see her now.

He descended the stairs and headed to the hospital. The place was in uproar with the men who could walk being sorted from those who needed to be carried. He spotted Barbara through the melee and strode through the tides of men.

She was with Dr Fayrer making notes as they assessed the state of the patients.

As he drew closer she turned in his direction. She was smiling for the first time in weeks. It made her even more beautiful. She spoke briefly to the doctor who glanced in his direction and took the notes from her.

She came over to him and took his arm. They stepped outside into the sunshine but their months of experience made them find the most sheltered spot.

"It's really happening?" she asked.

"I have seen them. They have heavy artillery on Faradays pulled by steam billies. They are taking apart any defence the enemy tries to put together."

She laughed and then cried.

"Wife of my heart," he said and embraced her.

"I can't believe it," she whispered.

"We must make plans," he said. "I will have to stay with the army. You will have to go with the civilians."

She sobbed. "I can't be parted from you," she cried. "How will I ever find you again?"

An artillery shell smashed into the hospital wall above them showering them with dust and lumps of stone.

"It's not over, my love."

"I'll stay with the troops," she pleaded. "I'll go with the doctor and be your nightingale."

He did not know what to say.

"Don't make me leave, Angus. I beg you."

He held her tighter. "I don't want to, Barbara, my sweet. But it's not my decision, nor is it yours. We have to obey orders."

She cried more and, if truth were to be told before God, his eyes stung with tears as well.

He took a deep breath. "Your family has business in Ceylon? In

Columbo?" He felt her nod. "Go there and wait for me. I promise I will come to you."

She pulled back a little and looked up into his eyes. "I will hold you to your promise, Lieutenant Ferguson. I will wait for you."

"I love you, wife of my heart."

"And I you, my husband."

Epilogue

Delhi, 1908

The taxi puttered to a halt at the entrance to the cemetery gate. The driver applied the brake and pulled a string that allowed the excess steam to jet into the air.

"Making heavy!" he shouted and flipped off the Faraday.

Then he jumped down from the front driving position and went around to the side door. Barbara had already got it open but allowed him to help her out and down. Her joints complained as she unfolded herself from the cramped compartment and out on to the street. It was hot, of course; Delhi was worse than Ceylon but there was a light breeze.

She should have gone to the Delhi Palace Hotel first to freshen up after the trip but she did not want to wait. Coming straight here from the air-dock was the sort of naïve and reckless thing she would have done fifty years ago.

The area was quiet. Indians preferred to cremate or otherwise dispose of their dead; they did not appreciate the British method of burying. It meant that their buildings did not crowd the British cemeteries the way they did everywhere else. And the closest Indian inhabitants were the lowest castes only.

"You wait for me," she ordered.

"Yes, *mem sahib*," he said and leaned against his vehicle in a way that was intended to indicate his capitulation to her instruction.

Barbara looked through the gates to the ranks of gravestones. So many men, and this was just the officers. Back then they did not give decent burials to the ordinary soldiers.

She opened her reticule and extracted the map. Another piece of paper fell out and she watched in horror as the breeze carried it away. The taxi driver was after it in a moment and snatched it out of the air. He returned it to her.

"Thank you."

It was a fragment of a newspaper and she pushed it back into her bag.

It took her fifteen minutes to reach the correct area of the cemetery and a further five minutes of tracking and back-tracking until she located the white stone that marked his grave.

Her deceased husband had a fancier stone than this and deserved it less. She had selected something appropriate for him and his position, but after the funeral she had never been back to it. And she never would. Their marriage of convenience had been convenient only to him and her father.

Ignoring the strain on her knees and back, she sat down beside the grave. All the grass was neatly tended, there were no weeds. A short distance away she could see that one grave had flowers. It was not such a surprise; fifty years had passed since these men had died retaking Delhi from the rebels. Few of them would have descendants that cared and how many of those would live in Delhi?

His name was etched into the stone though fifty years of heat and monsoon had worn it until it was barely visible. She reached out and ran her fingers along the letters. Then she opened up her reticule and extracted the newspaper clipping. She unfolded it and looked once more at the names of those who had been killed in the attack on the city. The ink had run in places where her tears had stained the paper.

She had been sitting at the breakfast table with her father. She scanned the newspaper for news desperately hoping she would not see his name but knowing that she must check. His name had leapt off the page at her. She had stifled a cry and run to her room. There she had beaten her hands against the wall and wept until there were no more tears. Fifty years ago.

Barbara wiped away a tear with her gloved fingers.

"My lovely man," she said quietly. "You did not come. And I was married."

Then she closed her eyes, remembered his face, felt his lips, and breathed in his kiss.

"I love you, Angus Ferguson."

~ end ~

Truth and Lies

The Siege of Lucknow is a real historical event which I have taken some liberties with while, I hope, not diluting the truth of what happened. There are several journals, both civilian and military, covering the siege and much of what's written here was derived from the diary of Selina Inglis.

The Indian Mutiny, as it was called by the British, was a complex issue but ultimately it came down to the attempt of the East India Company (that effectively owned India) to wipe out anything "non-British" through cultural imperialism.

The popular justification was that some rifle cartridges were supposedly prepared using pig-fat which meant that any Hindu, Muslim or Sikh soldiers handling them would be defiled. Whether this was true or not, it was a trigger in bringing about the rebellion.

After the rebellion, the East India Company was dissolved and all power and armies reverted to the British government who did, at least, make efforts to improve matters. I have tried to be fair and certainly do not condone what the EIC were doing. This story is, however, told from the viewpoint of those suffering under the siege.

Brigadier Inglis and his wife Selina were in charge of Lucknow after the death of Sir Lawrence, much in the way described here. Things would have turned out differently if someone less capable had been in charge.

The conditions in the Residency were appalling and the descriptions of death contained herein are a mere fraction of the horrors the people had to endure. Perhaps the worst part being that it was entirely possible for *anyone* to be killed simply walking from one part of the Residency to another. Whether by a musket ball, round shot (cannonball), shell or a falling building.

A strange event, after the siege, was that the ship carrying many of the survivors from Lucknow bound from Bombay (Mumbai) for England sank off Ceylon (Sri Lanka), though no one drowned. This is detailed in the account by Lady Selina Inglis (as she became).

Barbara Flynn, her mother, and Angus Ferguson are inventions, of course. Many of the events are pure fantasy while others are adaptations of real events. Barbara Makepeace-Flynn features in the Maliha Anderson books which take place some fifty years later (1908-1909). After the revelation that she had had an intense love affair when she was young, I felt the need to tell her story. And this is it.

In this alternate history, the Faraday device had only recently been invented (1843) so does not have a major influence on the story, or the events of the siege.

ABOUT THE AUTHOR

Steve Turnbull has been a geek and a nerd longer than those words have had their modern meaning.

Born in the heart of London to book-loving working class parents in 1958, he lived with his parents and two much older sisters in two rooms with gas lighting and no hot water. In his fifth year, a change in his father's fortunes took them out to a detached house in the suburbs. That was the year Dr Who first aired on British TV and Steve watched it avidly from behind the sofa. It was the beginning of his love of science fiction.

Academically Steve always went for the science side but he also had his imagination and that took him everywhere. He read through his local library's entire science fiction and fantasy selection, plus his father's 1950s *Astounding Science Fiction* magazines. As he got older he also ate his way through TV SF like *Star Trek*, *Dr Who* and *Blake's 7*.

However it was when he was 15 he discovered something new. Bored with a Maths lesson he noticed a book from the school library: *Cider with Rosie* by Laurie Lee. From the first page he was captivated by the beauty of the language. As a result he wrote a story longhand and then spent evenings at home on his father's electric typewriter pounding out a second draft, expanding it. Then he wrote a second book. After that he switched to poetry and turned out dozens, mostly not involving teenage angst.

After receiving excellent science and maths results he went on to study Computer Science. There he teamed up with another student and they wrote songs for their band - Steve writing the lyrics. Though they admit their best song was the other way around, with Steve writing the music.

After graduation Steve moved into contract programming but was snapped up a couple of years later by a computer magazine looking for someone with technical knowledge. It was in the magazine industry that Steve learned how to write to length, to deadline and to style. Within a couple of years he was editor and stayed there for many years.

During that time he married Pam (who also became a magazine editor) who he'd met at a student party.

Though he continued to write poetry all prose work stopped. He created his own magazine publishing company which at one point produced the subscription magazine for the *Robot Wars* TV show. The company evolved into a design agency but after six years of working very hard and not seeing his family—now including a daughter and son—he gave it all up.

He spent a year working on miscellaneous projects including writing 300 pages for a website until he started back where he had begun, contract programming.

With security and success on the job front, the writing began again. This time it was scriptwriting: features scripts, TV scripts and radio scripts. During this time he met a director Chris Payne, who wanted to create steampunk stories and between them they created the Voidships universe, a place very similar to ours but with specific scientific changes.

With a whole universe to play with Steve wrote a web series, a feature film and then books all in the same Steampunk world and, behind the scenes, all connected.